Nanny for the Bossy Daddy

Ava Nichols

Chapter 1

Haley

"I'm just sick and tired of getting my heart broken."

Sara nods sagely as I pace up and down the apartment. I've just moved in with her after I had to break my lease and move out of the place I shared with Reed, my ex-boyfriend.

"I can't believe that I let myself move in with this guy! I can't believe I let myself think he was different!"

"They're good at that kind of thing, babe," Sara points out from the couch. "They know all the right things to say."

I shake my head and continue to pace. "I know what it is. It's not just that, it's that I love bad boys and then I somehow expect them not to be bad to me. What kind of idiot does that? We're not fourteen anymore!"

"You wouldn't have liked me when I was fourteen," Sara observes, leaning back against the cushions.

"Good thing I met you in college, then." Sara was my college roommate and I'm glad that we stayed in touch because it meant I had a place to go when I caught Reed cheating on me.

Sure, I had to move to Seattle from Portland, but it's

Ava Nichols

fine. Honestly, the farther away I can get from my old life and my ex-boyfriend, the better I'll feel. This is a new city and a new start. I have to believe in that.

"I just have to stop dating," I announce.

"Uh...." Sara looks dubious.

"You don't think I can manage it?"

"I think that you... have a real weakness... and a certain type of guy knows what to say to get into your pants."

"I'm not talking about sex. A hookup is one thing. I mean actually falling for someone. These guys aren't worth my time, they treat me like crap, they cheat on me, and they don't care about what I want." I groan and flop onto the couch next to Sara. "I want to be a mother. That's what I want. And that's not going to happen as long as I'm dating these kinds of men."

"Actually, I think it's shocking it hasn't happened so far."

I glare at her. "Because I've been careful. I don't want to get pregnant when the dad's some jerk who cares more about his motorcycle than about helping pay the rent or doing the dishes. I want my kids to be raised by someone responsible. Not by a guy who can't even hold a steady job."

"Well, you're safe here." Sara takes my hand and squeezes it reassuringly, smiling. "I'm not going to let you start dating some other deadbeat, I promise."

"Thanks." I squeeze her hand in return. "I really appreciate it."

"Hey, you're helping me out, remember? I needed a roommate after the last one." Sara rolls her eyes. Her roommate saga has been a whole mess of its own.

While I'm not happy that my boyfriend cheated on me, breaking my heart yet again, I am grateful that it ended with me moving back in with Sara. I've missed her and this will, in some ways, be like being back in college. Except without the annoying exams and the finals-week crunch.

"I'm glad." I smile at her, and Sara smiles back.

Yeah, I hope this is the start of a new phase of my life. I don't want to end up like this again. I'm sick of finding someone who hits all my buttons and makes me weak in the knees, one of those bad-boy types that I so love... only to turn around three or six months later, or even a year later, and find that the person doesn't actually respect me, like Reed.

I'm going to wait and I'm going to find someone who actually treats me the way that I deserve.

Since I'm moving to a whole new city, I'm lucky that my job is in demand pretty much everywhere. Sara and I eat ice cream and drink wine, and enjoy our first night together as roommates after finishing moving me in. And the next day it's time to find a job.

I'm a nanny, which pays really well and allows me to spend time with kids, which is my favorite thing. I truly can't wait to be a mother. I've wanted to be one for the longest time. I've always gotten along well with kids and loved them. They're little people who are experiencing the world for the first time, and it's truly amazing. I mean that literally; it amazes me. The way that they interpret things. I don't understand how some people can be cruel to kids. This is all new to them and they need help.

I love helping them and being there for them as they explore it all. It brings me joy, and I think that parents can genuinely sense that, because I've never had a problem landing a job. As I scroll the job listings in Seattle, my eye falls on one in particular.

Full-time nanny wanted.

Must be willing to be with my child from breakfast until

bedtime. You will be compensated for your long hours, but your dedication must be genuine. Healthcare insurance benefits will be given by making you an employee of the parent's company, but vacation time will be strictly negotiated.

Odd. I mean, a nanny job where I could get insurance benefits from the employer, and I wouldn't have to go out and get my own insurance? That's a great benefit. But it sounds like they really want someone who might as well be a live-in nanny.

I hope it's okay that I'm not. I want to spend time with Sara and I'm not going to abandon her now that I've just moved in. She can't afford her apartment without another roommate covering half the bills.

I apply anyway since the amount they're offering to pay is insane. I'll be able to cover my month's expenses in just one week working for this person. I worry that the child in question is a brat, but it could be that the parents travel a lot, or one of the parents is ill, or something like that.

A couple of days later, I get a reply, and the woman and I agree to meet at a local coffee shop to discuss my experience and compatibility before I meet the kid.

The woman, Deborah, waves to me as I walk up. "Hi, are you Haley?"

"Hi, yes, and you must be Deborah." She's plus sized and curvy with dyed platinum blonde hair and a vintage style. She looks like she belongs in a 1950s magazine, and I mean that as a compliment. She's so well put together. "So, how many kids would I be watching? Just the one?"

"Yes, just Penny... Penelope, but we all call her Penny." Deborah smiles. "She's a really sweet girl, you'll like her."

"I'm sure I will." I might love kids, but in my experience, parents tend to really overestimate just how well-behaved their kids are, or how smart their kids are, and so on. I get it. When you love something that much it can be hard to be objective. "How old is she?"

"Five. Mr. Steele had another nanny for her; but unfortunately, the woman's husband just got a promotion across the country, so they're moving in a couple of weeks."

That brings me up short. "I'm sorry. You're not Penny's mother?"

Deborah blinks in surprise, then bursts out laughing. "Oh, no, I'm so sorry for the confusion! No, no, I'm Mr. Steele's personal assistant."

"Okay. Mr. Steele is in charge of hiring?"

"Yes, obviously. Well, technically I am, honestly; he's busy running the company. But it falls on me, yes. Mr. Steele is a single father."

Oh. "I'm so sorry."

Deborah nods briskly. "It is what it is. Penny needs a new nanny and I want to be sure I find someone who'll really give her the care and attention she needs. Mr. Steele won't be home much and his work has him traveling as well, but he wants the best for his daughter. Don't worry, you shouldn't be interacting with him much."

"But I'm nannying his daughter, so I assume I'll interact with him when he wants to spend time with her."

Deborah purses her lips. "Well, let's go over your credentials...."

The interview goes well, although I don't get a good impression of Mr. Jack Steele by the end of it. When I mention it to Sara, she says that she knows the name—he's in charge of some popular tech company in the area, I guess; and considered a very eligible bachelor, which was something I didn't think people cared about anymore outside of Regency romances.

Besides, I don't care how successful Mr. Steele is. I care that he doesn't seem to spend much time with his daughter and wants a nanny who will take care of everything instead.

I mean, really, who sends their personal assistant to interview the person who will be in charge of their child forty hours a week?

But that's not going to stop me from taking the job. The pay and the benefits are just way too good, and besides, Penny needs someone who cares about her, clearly. I'd be happy to be that person, at least for a while.

A couple of days later, I get a call from Deborah. "Congratulations, we'd love to hire you. Can you come by the office and I'll have you fill out all the paperwork?"

I take care of the paperwork first, just in case something last-minute happens to ruin it for me, and only then do I tell Sara when she gets home from work. I even buy one of those mini cakes from the supermarket.

"Ahhh!" Sara grabs me and hugs me tightly, continuing to scream. "We can't just enjoy this at home. Let's go out on the town and enjoy some bars! I know of a biker bar, and one that's got a rock band open mic night."

Those are exactly the kind of places I've been sneaking out to since I was sixteen, and maybe I should insist we stay home or at least go out to a respectable cocktail bar, but then I decide, why the hell not? And if I do meet a sexy man on a motorcycle... well, just because I make out with someone, or even sleep with them, doesn't mean I'm dating them.

We end up at the rock band bar and I'm having a blast. The music is loud, thumping through my body, but it's also good, and frankly, it isn't always in a rough-and-tumble place like this.

I head to the bar to grab another drink and end up slipping in some spilled alcohol, nearly falling over.

A strong arm comes around my waist, catching me. "Whoa there."

I look up and find that my savior from an embarrassing moment—especially with my skirt as short as it is—is an older man. He's going gray—silver in his temples and shot through his dark hair. His blue eyes are lively and sparkling with amusement and he's handsome as hell with a strong jawline. And oh God... I can feel his muscles and they're so damn firm.

He's even sporting a leather jacket. Fuck.

"You okay there?" My mystery man helps me stand upright.

"I'm great, thanks. Saved me a bruised ass." I laugh.

"If you want a bruised ass, there are much more fun ways to make that happen," my mystery man agrees, his voice low and sinful.

Oh fuck, that's hot. I shiver, my mouth going dry. "Very true." I look up at him through my lashes. I'm pretty sure he's flirting with me; and I suppose if I'm wrong, I can just find Sara and we can go to another bar where I can drown my sorrows over being embarrassed. "You want to help me with that?"

"Bold of you." My guy grins like a wolf and I almost whimper, my body lighting up inside. "I'm JJ."

"Haley." My voice comes out a squeak.

JJ chuckles and his hands fall to my hips... then lower, pulling me against him. I gasp as his large hands cup my ass. "That's a very short skirt you have on." His gaze drops down to my chest. "And a very low-cut shirt. Might make people think you're here for a particular reason."

"Maybe I am." My tongue sweeps out to wet my lips and I see JJ's gaze tracking the movement. "But only for the right person."

"Picky?"

"I like to call it having high standards."

"And do I meet your standards?"

"You're doing pretty well, so far."

JJ squeezes my ass. Normally, I'd be a little more concerned if this was a typical bar; but it's loud, there's a band playing, everyone's bumping against everyone else, and the bartender is doing body shots on a topless girl, so... pretty sure nobody cares if JJ hitches me up onto his broad, muscled thigh, while he massages my ass.

My hands grip his leather jacket and I melt against him. Oh, fuck, his thigh and his hands feel so good... and it's been so long since I had sex. Reed stopped having sex with me months ago and I just figured we were both so busy. Now, I know it's because he was fucking other women. I'm just glad he stopped having sex with me because who knows what I could've gotten from him if he hadn't.

JJ's looking at me like he's going to eat me alive, and I just might let him.

"Why don't I properly audition for the position," JJ murmurs, and then he takes my chin in his fingers and tips my face up, so he can slide his lips against mine.

He kisses me thoroughly, not just ramming his tongue into my mouth like so many men but teasing me with it until I'm panting, and only then does he let me have it. My knees give out, which only puts more of my weight on his thigh, and his grip on my ass while his other hand guides me to grind down against him.

I whimper. The drag of my clit against my panties and the tight denim of his jeans has me lighting up like a pile of fireworks. He's a good kisser, and so very in control, playing my body like he already knows all the ways to drive me insane.

He only pulls back when I'm panting and grinding desperately against his thigh. JJ smirks down at me. "Do I meet your standards?"

"Yes," I gasp out.

Fuck, yes, I'd kind of hoped for a good hookup to help me forget my jackass ex-boyfriend, but this is so much more than I'd ever expected.

"Then why don't we take this somewhere a little more private?"

I nod, my body thrumming with anticipation. The way JJ looks at me, like he's going to devour me, has my knees weak in a way I haven't felt in ages.

"What did you have in mind?" I'm not expecting a fancy hotel room with roses, and I wouldn't want one, but if he tries to take me back to some dirty trailer I'm going to have objections.

I'm trying to have higher standards for myself, damn it. Even if it's just with a one-night stand.

"Did you know this place has a back patio?"

"No." I grin. "I did not."

Sure enough, it does, and it's abandoned and empty. It's just a large awning with a bunch of picnic benches, and I see why the bar has it. During the warmer months it must be great to have the band perform out here instead, where you can fit more people. Some people can even probably pull up and park their motorcycles right along the side of it.

But right now, it's too chilly out to bother setting up out here, and everyone wants to be inside where the music is, or taking a cigarette break out in the front. It's just JJ and me.

JJ turns, his hands on my hips, walking backwards towards one of the picnic benches. It's one off to the side, in the shadow of the building, so that anyone who stumbles out here won't immediately see us.

9

"How much've you had to drink?" he asks, his voice low and amused.

"A couple shots. I like to stay alert."

"Mm, good girl."

His praise sends an electric thrill through me. The guys I've dated tend to talk to me in a very different way, calling me naughty, a bad girl, and sometimes getting kind of degrading. I always told myself that I liked it, that it came with the "bad boy" package, but JJ's praise lights me up like nothing I've really felt before.

I shove that thought into a corner of my brain. I'll think about it later, or not at all. I'm not here to have some kind of crisis, I'm here to have fun and celebrate my amazing new job.

"Don't worry. I know what I'm doing." It's sweet that he's checking to make sure I'm not too drunk.

"Good." JJ's smile turns wicked as he suddenly swings me around and presses me down onto the bench. "I want you able to *completely* feel what I'm doing to you."

I shiver with heat. JJ speaks with the kind of confidence that means I'm in for the time of my life.

His body presses me down, his hands slide up my arms to lightly pin my wrists to the table, his mouth lands on mine—and all thoughts fly out of my head.

I've never been kissed like this before. It's like JJ kisses with his entire body, putting everything into it, and I feel like I can't even breathe with the onslaught of his body on mine. His hands spread my legs and push up my short skirt, and then he's rocking against me, letting me feel his cock getting harder and harder under his jeans.

My greedy hands slide up under his shirt, feeling the bunching muscles of his back. Fuck, he's so fucking strong and muscled; how is this man real?

My fingers dig in and I gasp as JJ's mouth moves down to my throat, teasing me with his teeth against my skin. "F-fuck...."

I grind down against him, heat building in my body, especially between my legs. I want him inside of me, but unlike my previous hookups, JJ seems determined to take his time with me and really make me go crazy. I can't say that I mind, even as I squirm and pant for more.

This isn't like any hookup I've had before, and it makes my head spin, but it feels so good I don't want to stop. One of JJ's hands moves up under my low-cut shirt to my breast and the other moves between my legs to rub at me and I mewl, clawing at his skin under his own layers, panting, my nose filled with the scent of musk and leather.

He toys with my nipples and my clit like he wants to see just how badly he can drive me crazy, and I find myself slip-sliding into orgasm faster than I can believe it. "I'm—I'm going to—I'm gonna—"

He doesn't have to keep touching me. I'm so fucking wet for him, and I'm *aching*, wanting his cock inside of me. I can't remember the last time I was teased like this. Reed certainly never bothered. My addled brain tries to remember a time a man took the time to drive me crazy before fucking me, and maybe it's just that I'm so keyed up and turned on, but I can't think of any. After all, wasn't part of the point of finding some bad news with a leather jacket and a motorcycle the fact that you fucked fast and nasty in the bar bathroom?

But JJ, even as he mutters filthy things into my ear, seems perfectly happy to get me off before he gets inside me. It's almost... courteous. Considerate. Thoughtful.

It's also insanely hot.

His hand moves under the lace panties I put on, just in

11

case I got lucky, and the tip of his finger slides into me, just enough to tease before sliding back out. I gasp, and he does it again, then again, never moving in past the first knuckle.

"F-faster, deeper, please," I whisper as his mouth comes back up to meet mine for a bruising kiss.

"Aww, baby, am I not taking care of you enough?" JJ's tone is teasing, his voice deep and rough. He's completely in control, and it makes me shiver. "Have a little patience, sweetheart, enjoy the ride."

He slides his finger in a little more, then curls it up and strokes—*oh fuck.*

I let out a startled noise of pleasure and JJ chuckles. "You ever been with an older man before?"

"N-no. Oh God, oh my God, do that again, please—*oh.*" He does it more and I turn into a puddle, writhing, almost ready to come on just one goddamn finger.

JJ plucks and pinches at my nipple with his other hand. "Gotta say, a lot of the time those younger guys don't know what they're doing. They don't have the... *experience.*"

I believe him. He adds a second finger and keeps stroking that spot at that angle and my moans are getting louder—so much louder, in fact, that JJ has to take his other hand off my breast and put it over my mouth so that the people inside the bar don't hear me.

Not that he leaves my breasts alone. Now that he's got my shirt all pushed up, he can put his mouth on them instead. He licks and sucks and scrapes his teeth over my nipples like he's starving, and I'm helpless, caught between his fingers and his mouth, screaming my pleasure into the palm of his hand.

JJ speeds up his fingers. "There we go, c'mon, you're so close, I can feel it... come for me... c'mon, baby girl...."

His thumb rubs at my clit and that's it. I come so hard

I'm almost embarrassed, sobbing and squirming. My vision blurs and I feel completely out of control of my body as I'm wracked with pleasure. Holy fuck, holy fuck, holy *fuck*. I didn't know it was even possible to come that hard.

"Christ, you're so fucking hot. Look at you. Gorgeous. Such a good girl for me." JJ's praise has me glowing.

He pulls back and stands up, undoing his pants, and a shiver of heat runs through me again. I just came, the aftershocks shaking my body, but I'm still needy. I want him to fuck me. If that's what he can do to me with his fingers, I'm desperate to know what he'll do with his cock.

JJ pulls his cock out and rolls on a condom. My mouth waters. I push myself up and lean in, mouthing at it, licking up and down the shaft. JJ groans, his hand sliding into my hair.

"Such a good girl, showing initiative." Wow, I am really into how he talks to me, all purring praise. "That's it, get it nice and wet so I can fuck you—oh, fuck yes."

I suck at the head of his cock, just a little bit, just the tip, and JJ growls. "Don't be a tease or I'll slide the whole thing down your throat."

I moan instinctively and he smirks. "Yeah, you like it a little rough, huh? Tempting. Very tempting. But not tonight. I want to get inside you."

I pull back and spread my legs out, pushing one of my knees up. "Please."

JJ chuckles and crawls over me, settling between my thighs. I can feel the head of his cock nudge up against my entrance. "Hold on."

He takes off his jacket, revealing firm, broad, muscled arms. I can feel my eyes go wide. He could probably pick me up one-handed, no problem.

Ava Nichols

JJ folds his jacket and puts it under my head, then hands me the sleeve of it. "Bite down on that, okay?"

I nod. It's a smart idea, since I don't know if I'll be able to keep quiet, but the idea of having his leather jacket in my mouth is also insanely hot. It's also very sweet of him to think to use it as a cushion for my head.

We haven't even finished the sex yet, and JJ's already the most courteous guy I've ever hooked up with.

Then he slides inside of me and all thoughts are just pushed right out of my head.

I have to bite down on the jacket sleeve immediately, the taste of leather flooding my mouth, as a cry escapes me. JJ braces his hands on either side of my head and fucks me hard and fast, and just a little rough, but not like he's just using me as a hole. A lot of guys can fuck rough and fast, but not a lot of them can do it with actual technique, and JJ seems to know exactly the angle and speed to have me screaming around the leather and jerking my hips up to meet his thrusts.

My brain feels like it's goo, and actually so does my spine, as I whimper and my vision blurs. I can't even grab on to him properly; my hands go limp, my fingers twitch, and my body is out of control with pleasure. I didn't know it was possible for my body to feel this amazing. It's like he's found three different spots I didn't know existed and all of them make my body light up.

JJ groans and drops onto his elbows, kissing along my neck. "You feel so fucking good, sweetheart, *fuck.*"

He speeds up, somehow fucking me even faster, and everything turns into white-hot uncontrollable pleasure. My legs jerk up, wrapping around JJ's waist, wanting him closer, deeper, wanting more and more and more of that almost unbearable ecstasy—

I moan as he stops, buried deep inside of me, and rolls his hips. It feels so good, but I was so close, why—why did he stop—

"Fuck, you feel so good. Can't let this be over too soon. You're so hot—so tight—" JJ pulls out and thrusts hard and rough a few more times, and then buries himself in me and stops again, rolling his hips, his cock completely inside of me and just dragging over and over against those spots of pleasure.

He repeats it a few more times, the start and stop of it driving me insane. I claw at him mindlessly, my hips jerking up in desperation. I need to come, I'm right on the edge and I know I could go over if he would just stop *toying* with me.

And yet, I don't want it to end. This is the best sex I've ever had in my life. This is pleasure I didn't know I could feel, and part of me doesn't want it to ever stop.

Finally, JJ seems to give in to his own desperation. He swears through gritted teeth and fucks me with abandon, wild and animalistic, and the feeling of it—I can't stop myself, I can't control it—I go right over the edge.

My orgasm takes me by surprise. I've been almost there for so many minutes that I almost forgot that I could spill over. I can feel tears sliding down my face as I come, the feeling so fucking good that I can't hold it in and I have to literally cry about it. That's never happened to me before. I've heard from other girls about *"coming so good I cried,"* but I figured it was just an exaggeration, because how could you ever have an orgasm that good?

Turns out I was wrong. It's fully possible, if you're with a man who knows what he's doing.

JJ grunts and comes, hard; and I can feel it inside of me even with the condom on. I have a sudden flash of desire for there to be nothing between us; for him to fill me up with

15

his hot, sticky spend; and to feel an aftershock of orgasm roll through me. That would be so dirty and naughty. I've never given in to that fantasy, for health reasons, but fuck....

We pant together, both basking in the power of our climax. Fuck.

Eventually, JJ pulls the sleeve out of my mouth and lazily kisses me, almost like it's a *thank you*. "How do you feel?"

"Mmm. Amazing." I grin up at him. "Thanks for that."

"Well, you weren't so bad yourself." JJ winks at me and then pushes himself up, sliding out of me.

He disposes of the condom and tucks himself back in, then helps me set my clothes back right. Unfortunately with my short skirt, I think it's a bit ruined. I tie JJ's jacket around my waist for the time being.

"I'll get you a drink at the bar and then we can get you to your car so nobody sees." It's once again more thoughtful than any of my previous hookups or boyfriends have been. JJ doesn't want me to feel embarrassed or to get comments, and I appreciate it, but anyone else I've been with didn't care or thought it was funny.

I really don't know what to do with being treated so well. "Thank you."

"No problem."

We head back inside, and JJ leads me to the bar with his hand on the small of my back. He has such a commanding presence, even with everyone caught up in the music from the band, they sense him and move out of the way, parting like the Red Sea. It makes me shiver.

"One whiskey sour," JJ orders, then passes me some napkins so I can discreetly clean myself up. His body blocks me from others and I can take care of things under his jacket. Once I'm finished, I hand his jacket back.

"Thank you."

"Don't mention it."

"There you are!" Another guy slides over and claps JJ on the shoulder. "Geez, JJ, we've been looking for you everywhere. One of the bassists from the last band wanted to talk to you."

"You play music?" I ask.

"This guy is one of the best I ever met," JJ's friend assures me. "Our band—"

"She doesn't want to hear about the band."

"Of course I want to hear about the band." I know that indie performers need all the help they can get. "Hey, could I get—"

I'm about to say *your CD* or something like that—even in this day and age, with Bandcamp and Spotify, bands will have demo CDs to hand out to people—but JJ's face shuts down faster than I can blink, growing cold and impassive.

"No, thank you," he says, and it's so different from the charming and courteous, sexy man I just fucked, that I literally take a step back in shock.

JJ looks at his friend. "Yeah, I'll see that bassist," he says, and then he practically drags his friend away from me without a second glance.

What... what the fuck was that?

Chapter 2

Jack

Damn it, and things were going so well with Haley too.

That was the best sex I've had in a long while. I try to remember better sex that I've had and while I'm sure that I must have, I can't remember it in the moment. Haley clearly wasn't used to praise or to a man who knows what the hell he's doing in the bedroom.

I'm more than happy to show her what it's like when a man who knows what he's doing has access to her gorgeous body.

And she is gorgeous. I stepped in to grab her when she slipped, not even really thinking about it other than wanting to help someone who might fall and get hurt, but the moment she was in my arms I realized just how beautiful she is. She's got a pert ass and small pert breasts, the kind that I want to get my teeth on; curly shoulder-length dark hair that I want to dive my fingers into and tug; warm, light brown skin that's soft to the touch; and sparkling green eyes that I could stare into for days.

She looks exactly like the kind of pretty girl you want to mess up and ruin, and that's exactly what I do.

It sets my blood on fire when I find out that she's a screamer, and the best part is she seems shocked about it. It's so damn clear to me that Haley's never had a guy actually give her a good enough time. I'd bet my entire damn fortune that she's had nothing but mediocre sex to the point where she had no idea that it was mediocre and thought it was nice and good, and maybe even great.

Well, now I get to show her exactly how good sex really feels.

And fuck, it's not like I have a bad time, either. She's gorgeous, she feels amazing, she sounds amazing.... I end up dragging it out longer, just so that it doesn't have to end; I'm just that fucking into her body and her reactions.

I have no problem with having fun with a woman. I've had a lot of fun with a lot of women over the years, in fact. But this is so much more. It's been a while since I slowed the sex down to drag it out for both of us, but I need it, knowing the climax when it comes will be so much better.

And I'm absolutely right. I have to bite down on my own tongue so I don't make some loud damn noise myself.

I almost wish that I could break my own rule and get her number so that I can see her again, and have some more great sex, but I don't think that's a good idea. Every time I think that I've found someone who understands it's just sex, I'm wrong. Women always ask me for more, and I can't give it to them.

I've learned to just shut it down immediately and leave it at that. Better to walk away from something than to try and get my hopes up. I'm not ever going to give another woman my heart, not after I lost my wife, Emily. I've been

19

through the pain of that and I will never put myself through that again.

And then, Haley ruins it. I wanted to have a drink with her, chat with her, and then make sure she met up with whoever she came here with or get her a ride home, whatever she needed... send her off safely. But Mark comes up and interrupts us, and that's when Haley tries to ask me for my number.

Goddammit.

I can hear the excitement and hope in her voice, and I shut it down immediately. No way. No matter how much Haley promises me that she understands it's just sex, she'll hope for more, especially when she finds out how rich I am. That's always how it goes.

So I shut it down, and I walk away.

Mark frowns and glances over his shoulder as I drag him away from the bar and Haley. "Did I interrupt something?"

"Don't worry about it."

"She looked upset."

"She's used to men disappointing her; she'll get over it." She's young, anyway. I don't know how much younger she is than I am, but I'm guessing late twenties. Plenty of time to get over a random hookup being rude to her.

Mark looks like he might say something else, but then he sighs and introduces me to the young bassist who wants to talk to me.

It's a pleasant surprise that the guy's genuinely interested in my advice, and not just doing it out of politeness because Mark insisted. Of my three former bandmates, Mark's the one who's never really given up on the idea of us playing together.

Now that we're all in our forties, of course, there isn't really a chance of us doing it professionally anymore and making it big. That was our dream, back in college, and I think we were good enough to maybe actually make something of it. But Mark still wants us to actually play regularly again, even if it's just for fun.

I can't do that. I have a company to run, and a large one. You don't get to be a billionaire, especially in the fast-paced world of tech, by resting on your laurels.

But it's nice to go out every once in a while and enjoy listening to some good rock music, support up-and-comers, people who are young and hungry like we once were.

I finish giving the bassist advice, and Mark smiles at me as the kid walks off to rejoin his bandmates. "You remember when we were like that?"

"God, yeah."

"You miss it." Mark bumps me on the shoulder. "Tell me you don't, go on, try and lie to me."

"Mark, we're parents now. You're married. So is Eli. Steve and his girlfriend are getting serious and you know he's always wanted to adopt; that process can take years. We don't have time—"

"Just for fun!" Mark rolls his eyes. "Come on, we could own a place like this, we'd have the crowd eating out of the palms of our hands."

"That was two decades ago."

I know that Mark won't be deterred. He hasn't been deterred the entire time. When I first decided to get serious and start my tech company for Emily, my girlfriend at the time, I knew I wouldn't have time for the band, and I wasn't going to screw over my girlfriend or my bandmates by committing halfway to both of them.

But then Emily left me, and Mark thought he had a chance to convince me to give up my company. At that point, though, I'd invested far too much. Emily's ideas had been brilliant, and I'd had the business knowledge, and even though Emily had been gone, I couldn't give up on the company that I'd poured everything into.

When she'd come back years later, I'd felt rewarded. Like I made the right decision.

Now that she's gone, I wonder, sometimes.

But it doesn't matter. I have a billion-dollar company to run and I can't go galivanting off to play guitar with my friends like I'm in high school and operating out of someone's mom's garage. I have to travel constantly, I have a million things to keep track of. And my bandmates have responsibilities of their own. Hell, I'm the only single one.

Mark just talks a big game. He doesn't actually have the ability or time to pursue our old dreams. That's just how life works. Sometimes, you make a choice, and then that choice leads you down a certain path.

You can't go back, even if sometimes, you really wish you could.

Mark rolls his eyes at me. "You're a spoilsport. But c'mon, let's find Eli and Steve, I think they snagged a pool table."

I follow Mark to the pool table and let myself get swept up in the company of my closest friends, and I forget all about Haley.

The next morning, I'm up early. No matter how late I stay up, I have to be awake on time so that I can run the company. Deborah, as expected, is in the foyer when I come downstairs.

"Someone looks like they were up late," she notes.

"Is that your way of telling me I look like shit?"

"I would never say such a thing out loud, sir," Deborah tells me blithely.

Deborah has been my personal assistant for years and

she's the only person who can really get away with talking to me like this and teasing me. She keeps me steady and grounded, and while I'll never admit it out loud, or I'll never hear the end of it from her, in some ways she's my best friend.

I head into the kitchen to grab some coffee before I head to the office, but unlike usual, Deborah isn't saying anything about the rest of my day. She's not filling me in on meetings or telling me the various plans or reminding me about a luncheon.

I frown at her as I turn on the coffee machine. I make a coffee for her too. "Something wrong?"

Deborah sighs. "Did you forget, sir?"

"Forget what?" I wrack my brain. "Don't tell me I'm supposed to be on a plane somewhere."

"No. You're supposed to meet the new nanny for Penny."

Ah, damn, I did forget all about that. "Well—"

The doorbell rings. Deborah gives me a stern *behave* look. "That'll be her. Try to act like you're excited to meet her."

"If you picked her out then I trust that she'll take good care of Penny." My daughter gets only the best. It's the least I can do for Emily.

Deborah opens the door and smiles. "Haley, great to see you again, come on in."

The name has my stomach flipping over. Surely that's a fairly common name, right? There's no need to think—

Then the nanny steps inside, and *oh fuck.*

Yeah. That's *my* Haley.

The woman I fucked last night.

Shit.

Chapter 3

Haley

J ack and Penny Steele live in a stunning home that looks like it's a part of the forest that surrounds it. As I pull up the drive, I can't see any of the houses around it, making it feel secluded. There's an almost fairy-tale feel to it that makes it feel magical.

I wonder what it would be like to grow up in a place like this. It seems amazing.

As I park the car in the massive driveway, I note that I'll have to take full advantage of the outdoors here in playing with Penny. I'm sure that she'll love it. Kids these days are so tempted by electronics and I can't blame them; aren't we all? And so many parents just let them be. It's so hard to avoid getting a kid addicted to electronics nowadays as people's lives move more and more online.

I want to help Penny spend time in real life, outside, the way I was able to as a kid.

Taking a deep breath, I get out of the car.

I admit, the way that JJ suddenly went cold on me last night didn't help my self-esteem. I don't know what I did wrong, and I don't think it bodes well for my attempt to pick better men for myself.

But I have to push that all aside today. My ability to be a great nanny to Penny has nothing to do with my choices in men. I can do this.

I just really hope that her father likes me and doesn't fire me on the spot.

I walk up and knock on the door. I dressed up just a little, wearing a dress instead of jeans and a shirt, wanting to impress on my first day.

Deborah opens the door, smiling at me. "Haley!"

I melt a little in relief when I see her. I'm so glad that it won't be me just meeting Jack Steele on my own. Deborah made him seem like a pretty tough guy and I admit I'm intimidated to meet him.

I step inside and turn as Deborah says, "Mr. Steele, this is Haley, she's the person I hired as Penny's new nanny."

And my heart just about stops.

Because standing there, staring at me in shock, is JJ.

I swallow. What do I do? This can't be right. I need to pay my bills, I can't have this amazing job turn out to be something I have to quit because I accidentally slept with my boss.

I can feel my face heating up. I feel absolutely humiliated. Whatever went wrong last night, I don't know, but it has to have made a bad impression. Now Jack Steele, JJ, is going to be my *boss* and he's going to fire me on the spot.

Jack straightens up, and I feel as if I can see some kind of mask or curtain settling over his face. "Haley. It's nice to meet you."

His tone is stiff and formal, cold, completely unlike the charming man that I spoke to and had sex with last night. I can't imagine this man stepping out to help a woman keep from falling, or flirting so brazenly with someone.

"Penny should be in her room," Jack continues. "In her wing of the house."

Shock floods me and makes me temporarily forget to be embarrassed. "Her wing of the house?"

I look at Deborah, who nods in confirmation. "Penny and Mr. Steele keep their own schedules."

I look back at Jack. "So you don't go and see her? At all?"

"Why should I? That's what I'm hiring you for. I'm a busy man, I have a company to run. That's why I have you, to take care of my daughter."

I know I'm staring, but I can't help it. "What the hell is wrong with you?" I blurt out.

Deborah struggles to hide a snort behind a cough. Jack arches an eyebrow and takes a sip of whatever fancy coffee is in his black mug. "Excuse me?"

"I asked what's wrong with you. Do you not care about your daughter at all?"

I fold my arms. If I'm already going to be fired for sleeping with my boss, I don't see what I have to lose by dressing him down a bit. And I refuse to let any kid be ignored like this by their parent if I can help it. "I've nannied for a lot of parents who are too busy to spend time with their kids, and the kids are always upset about it. I'm not a replacement for being a parent; I'm an additional parent, I'm a help, I'm assistance."

"No." Jack's voice stays mild. "You're whatever I pay you to be. And if I want you to take care of my daughter, that's what you're going to do, unless you don't want the job."

"Unless *I* don't want the job?" I scoff. "Right. As if you're going to keep me around."

"Do you have this attitude with all of your employers?"

"Just the jackasses," I snap.

I'm not sure why he hasn't fired me on the spot yet. Deborah looks both shocked and amused.

Jack sips his coffee. It's infuriating. It's like he thinks I'm just some sort of... child having a temper tantrum and he has to just wait me out.

"Do you have nothing to say?" I ask. "Or are you just going to keep staring at me like a moron? I worried when I was hired and spoke to your personal assistant, but this is ridiculous."

"I don't see what there is that needs to be said. You're not going to change anything. If you can't accept the job, then fine, I'll have Deborah hire someone else and you can just babysit Penny for the day while she finds someone to replace you. But otherwise, I expect you to just do the job you were hired for, and that's looking after my daughter. You can take it or leave it."

He's so damn cold and impersonal and *arrogant*. I'm honestly shocked. I've never had anyone behave like this in my life, not even when I was in college and waiting tables and dealing with spoiled jerks on a regular basis.

I can't lie, I'm tempted to walk out the door. I don't want to deal with such an asshole. I can't believe that I slept with this guy... and yet at the same time I can. I thought I'd finally picked someone who actually was a good person. A "bad boy" in the way that I liked but also someone who wouldn't treat me like crap.

And yet I was wrong again. I just didn't realize until after I'd already slept with the guy.

Great. Just great.

But as much as I want to walk away from this absolute disaster, I can't walk away from a child who needs someone to love them. I can't imagine that Penny gets any kind of proper love from this man standing in front of me.

Maybe I'm just setting myself up for a migraine. But if the job really is unbearable, I can always find another. Nannies are always needed, especially among the rich, and Seattle has plenty of those. I just... I can't walk away from a lonely little girl. I can't.

I haven't even met Penny yet, and I care about her.

My jaw clenches. "I'm staying. Not for you or for whatever money you want to throw at me. I see now why you're financially compensating me so well, it's to make up for having to deal with you. I'll stay because I'm sure your daughter is lovely, and if you can't see that, then it's your loss."

I turn to Deborah. "Could you show me through this monstrosity to where Penny's wing of the house is?"

I still like the house. The inside is as beautiful as the outside, continuing this woodland and nature theme, with beautiful wood beams in the ceiling and a lovely green carpet that gives you the feeling of standing in the lush grass on the forest floor.

But no way am I letting Jack know that I like anything that I think he has a hand in.

Deborah looks back and forth between Jack and me, and then nods. "Okay, I'll... lead you to her."

I don't even give Jack a second glance.

"I'm surprised he didn't just fire me," I whisper. "Why am I not fired?"

"Probably because he's impressed you stood up to him," Deborah replies. "He won't ever admit it, but he likes it when someone has the guts to do it. He's surrounded by yes-men all the time, all rich men are."

"Well, if he expects me to mellow out towards him, he's got another thing coming," I mutter.

"I hope you'll stick around," Deborah confides. "I've never liked how he keeps his daughter at arm's length, but it's one of the few things I've never been able to discuss with him. Maybe you'll change his mind. Who knows?"

"Fat chance of that," I snort.

Judging by the way he dismissed me so abruptly, the minute his friend showed up, I don't think Jack is going to listen to me about anything.

But if I'm going to quit or going to get fired, we'll find out soon. Right now, I try to shove the horrible father out of my mind and focus on the kid, and meet Penny.

The door that leads to her bedroom has her name written on it in letters made out of woodland animals. It's adorable.

Deborah knocks on the door. "Penelope, it's time to get up. Your new nanny is here."

She opens the door and ushers me in.

The room is done up in soft blues and greens, and the bed is shaped like a sailboat. Penny is sitting up in bed, her hair a tangle of red curls, and she's reading a picture book.

She looks up as we enter and Deborah smiles. "Penny. If you're up should you be reading?"

Penny shakes her head.

"What are you supposed to do first?"

"Get dressed?"

"Exactly. Penny, this is Haley, she's going to be your new nanny."

"Hi, Penny." I step forward and crouch in front of her. "It's really great to meet you. I'm Haley."

"Hi, Haley." Penny looks me up and down. "You're prettier than my last nanny."

I burst out laughing while Deborah groans. "Penny, please."

Penny shrugs. "It's the truth!"

"That's sweet of you to say I'm pretty, but maybe we need to work on how we compliment people." I grin. "I like you already. What do you say we get some breakfast and spend the day getting to know each other?"

Penny nods.

She doesn't seem as shy as some kids I've worked with, but she doesn't seem super friendly and eager, either. She's a bit calmer than I'd like. If that's how she is naturally, that's fine, but I worry that she's so calm and accepting because her dad's put her through a lot of nannies in her life.

I'm just another adult who's going to take care of her for a bit and then disappear.

I swallow hard. I'm lucky to have such a good relationship with my parents, and I know that not every kid is so lucky. Jack might be amazing at sex and charming when he wants to be, and I'm sure he's a good and respected businessman or he wouldn't have gotten so damn rich. But he's not a good father, and I have every intention of letting him know it.

If he doesn't want to fire me because I stand up to him, then fine. I'll keep standing up to him. Maybe at some point, he'll listen.

But first things first: bonding with Penny.

"I don't know about you," I whisper to her, "but one of my favorite things for breakfast is blueberry pancakes. Do you think we could have those?"

Penny smiles. "I like blueberry pancakes too."

"Fantastic." I hold out my hand. "C'mon, kiddo, think

you can show me where the kitchen is? I'm so lost in this big house!"

Penny giggles and gets out of bed, taking my hand.

Yeah, I'm going to shower this girl in affection. I can't wait to see her smile like that all the time.

Chapter 4

Jack

The entire car ride to work, I debate whether or not I should keep Haley on.

I had sex with her. Before I knew who she was, or she knew who I was, but it could still be a problem. A conflict of interest.

But... I don't like the idea of firing someone just because I couldn't keep it in my pants and made the wrong choice. She's my employee *now*, and so I can keep my distance.

It's not like I'm going to fuck her again. Not after everything that's just happened.

No, if she's going to get fired, it's because we can't stand each other. I'm shocked that the woman I liked so much last night is yelling in my face the next morning, but it's not like I got where I am in life by being the nicest guy in the room. I got where I am in life by being the smartest, or most creative, or sometimes the most ruthless guy in the room.

Penny is the daughter of the woman I loved, and so she deserves the best. I'm impressed that Haley had no problem standing up to me even if it meant she lost her job, and I like that she's already so passionate about my daughter when she hasn't met her.

I'm sure that Haley will get along with Penny. I liked Haley last night, and I don't see any reason why my daughter won't either.

And I really don't want to have Deborah search for a replacement. If Deborah thinks that Haley is the best person for the job, then I trust my assistant's choice. And I need her to be helping me, I can't have her wasting time interviewing more people.

This will be fine. Haley and I had sex; it didn't mean anything; in fact, I don't want it to mean anything, so frankly this is nothing according to how I conduct my own sex life. There's no reason for me to be upset or anxious. I'm not going to treat her worse or better because we had sex once. I never thought I'd see her again, after all.

We just have to find a way to get along as employer and employee.

I head into work feeling calmer about the situation. It's going to be fine. Haley already cares about Penny and she's not in awe of me like so many are. She came with amazing recommendations and experience, and my assistant likes her. I'm barely around Penny anyway, so I'm sure I'll barely see her.

And yet, somehow. That is not what happens.

I'm right about Haley and Penny bonding. Penny adores Haley and is soon as close with her as she was with her last nanny, which is a relief. Our last nanny stayed with us the longest and I had hoped she'd be with us for a few more years, until Penny was old enough to have more independence.

But then her husband got that promotion and off they went. It was a disappointment, for sure, but I can't blame her for not even thinking twice about it. He's her spouse. What else is she going to do, stay here? My daughter's great but not that great, no kid is that's not your own.

I worried that nobody would be able to be a good replacement in Penny's life, but she and Haley get along great.

Haley and I on the other hand....

Somehow, I run into her more often than I ever did the previous nannies. I go into the kitchen to get a coffee, and she's in there making a meal for Penny. I go out onto the patio at the end of the work day to relax, and she and Penny are playing in the backyard.

Every time I turn around, Haley's there.

It's bad enough when she's with Penny. I try to avoid my daughter as much as I can because it's just too painful to see her. She looks so much like her mother, with Emily's curls and heart-shaped face.

Emily was supposed to raise Penny with me. She was supposed to be our daughter, our dream come true. And instead, Emily never even got to meet her.

It's better that I keep my distance from her. Better that I be absent than infect her with my grief.

But without Penny there as a buffer, Haley and I go from cold cordiality to outright hostility.

You'd think I never gave her a good orgasm for how she seems to find me unable to do anything right.

Sometimes I want to snap at her *you realize I made you orgasm twice, right?* But that would be childish and wildly inappropriate. She's driving me crazy, but I'm not going to hold what we did against her in any way.

But Haley makes it clear, day in and day out, that she doesn't approve of my keeping a distance from my daughter, and she never ceases to find an opportunity to bring it up.

"Penny's doing great in kindergarten," she notes. "You should see the pictures she drew of dinosaurs. They learned all about them today."

Another time, I find Penny's homework assignments, finished and with gold stars on them, put on the desk at my home office.

Haley has my email, and technically Deborah should be handling these first, but I think she's getting a kick out of how annoyed Haley makes me; so I find emails in my inbox with pictures and videos of things Penny did with her during the day.

"Stay out of my personal office," I inform Haley the next day she shows up for work in the morning. "It's off-limits."

I lock it, just to be sure.

Haley somehow learns to pick the locks, because there's still stuff on my desk the day after.

I get another lock.

Haley can't seem to learn how to pick that one, so she instead tapes the homework and drawings to the closed office door or slides them underneath.

Okay, fine, there is something amusing about her attempts. She's determined and cheeky about it. Who the hell learns how to pick a lock just to annoy their boss with cute pictures a little kid drew? Haley, apparently.

I can't help but be reluctantly impressed. I'm a businessman who built his billion-dollar company up from nothing. Of course I'm going to respect someone who has the moxie to push her agenda. It's what I had to do. I had so many doors slam in my face when I first started out, but I didn't let it deter me. I just kept going.

The thing is, Haley may be stubborn, but she's not as stubborn as I am. I've also learned what it's like to be on the other side of the table. I've learned patience. And it's none of her business how I choose to raise my daughter.

I'm paying her to nanny, and that's what she needs to focus on. That's it. Full stop.

I will say it is... refreshing to have someone so unafraid of me. Only my old bandmates sass me like this anymore. They're the only people who knew me before I was rich, before all of the power. They remember when I was just a gangly idiot freshman banging it out on an ancient guitar in one of the music rooms at our college.

I just wish I could figure out a way for us to get along.

Haley's been Penny's nanny for about a month when I get home one day to find Haley's car parked not in the driveway or in one of the parking spaces, but in the middle of the road. She's on the phone standing next to it, leaning back against the hood, and she looks miserable.

"Okay. All right. Yes, thank you."

I pull up and roll down the window. "What's wrong?"

"Mr. Steele."

"Jack." I've told her to call me that dozens of times and she never listens. I don't like being called Mr. Steele outside of work—well I don't like it at all, but I get it's necessary and respectful—it makes me feel like I'm my stuffy father.

Although I'll never admit it to Mark, because he'll never let it go, I do sometimes look at myself in the mirror, at this clean-cut guy, and wonder what happened to the tattooed rebel who wanted nothing more than to shred on the guitar.

"Mr. Steele," Haley repeats, because she seems to have figured out that I don't like being called that, and she lives to spite me, apparently. "I'm so sorry about this. I took Penny to the museum today and my car broke down right here. Don't worry, she's inside the house, I made her dinner and got her some coloring books."

"Don't worry about it. I know you wouldn't let anything happen to her." Haley's devotion to Penny was instant and is pretty absolute. If it wasn't, I doubt she'd be bothering me constantly about her. "What's wrong with the car?"

"I'm not sure. I knew that there was something iffy with it, the check engine light came on a week ago, but I've just been so busy I kept putting it off. I know you're strict about me taking days off and I just kept forgetting to go after work."

I do have Haley practically living here. I don't want to be in charge of Penny while I'm trying to work at home, and that's when I even *am* home. I work long hours and I'm not often around. I'd never leave Penny alone at this age. I hope when she's older she can spend time after school with friends instead, and a nanny won't be practically a 24/7 thing like she needs while she's still so young.

"Don't worry about it. You called a tow truck?"

"Yes." She grimaces. "It'll take them a bit to get out here, though."

"Not a problem. And I'll pay for it."

Haley, for some reason, glares daggers at me when I say that. "No, you won't."

"Yes, I will."

"I can afford to pay for my own tow truck with what you pay me, Mr. Steele. I don't need your charity."

"Charity? Your car is broken down in the middle of the road because I work you so much that you didn't have time to take it to the garage. Paying for a tow truck is the least I can do."

"No, you just want to try and swoop in and be the hero so you'll get on my good side and I'll let up about your relationship with Penny. I'm not some charity case and I'm certainly not some woman you can... buy off."

37

I groan and get out of the car. "Haley. I'm not trying to buy my way into your affection. You've made it pretty clear where you stand. Just let me help you out. Do you need a ride home tonight?"

"I was going to call my roommate to pick me up."

"Right. And how much of an inconvenience would that be for her?"

Haley opens her mouth, then closes it. She doesn't look happy.

Damn, she's gorgeous when she's pissed off. I know I shouldn't be thinking that, since she's my employee, but I'm not going to do anything about it. It's just a simple fact. Haley's damn gorgeous, and I apparently love seeing her all riled up in anger just as much as I love seeing her riled up from me teasing her body.

"Your roommate's going to have to drive forever out of her way to get you. And let me guess, you'll insist on paying her for the gas too. Let me pay for the tow truck and drive you home. Out of the two of us, I'm the one with an insane amount of money to burn, so let me burn it. I make it faster than I can give it away, all right?"

She looks at me for a long moment, and I think she's going to say no again, that her stubbornness is going to win out—but then she slumps back against the car and sighs.

"Fine. But will you have someone to watch Penny while you drive me? She shouldn't be in the car for so long, not right after dinner. She needs to be winding down for bed."

"Fair enough." I have some neighbors I can call to just stay with her, an older couple that have some grandkids around Penny's age. "I'll make sure someone's with her."

I call the neighbors and get that set up, the tow truck guy arrives, and once everything's settled, Haley and I get into the car for me to drive her home.

38

She gives me her address, I put it into the navigation system, and from there we have the most awkward silent car ride I've ever been on in my life, and I've taken a lot of rideshares in my time as I travel for work.

Haley stares out the car window, apparently uninterested in having any kind of conversation, even an argument, and I follow her lead. It's no problem for me. I have various work emails that I have my car AI read out to me and do speech-to-text in response, so I'm not losing out on any work by driving her.

We're almost there when Haley says, "Does it ever stop?"

"What?"

"The emails. The texts. The work."

"Not when you're a CEO. Or at least, not when you're a CEO who actually cares." I frown, thinking of a few lazy sons of bitches I could name. "There are a lot of C level executives who don't do any work, just reap the benefits. They can afford to pay their workers so much more, the guys who do the actual work, and instead they just take all they can and sit around and make a couple decisions a year. They're off playing golf all the time."

"Wow, such anger in your voice over the golf."

"I hate golf. It's boring. But everyone wants to play it, and so they end up having these business deals out on the green, so I gotta go or I get shut out of shit."

"Poor baby," Haley says dryly. "You have to go and hit a little ball around on the grass. How difficult for you."

I roll my eyes to hide the fact that I want to chuckle. Haley's sass is amusing, I like it, and I like that she's not scared of me. She has zero problem telling me like it is. I'm so damn tired of being surrounded by "yes men." At least Haley dislikes me to my face instead of pretending to fawn all over me and then saying shit about me when I'm not in the room.

You'd think that rich businessmen could afford to act less like they're gossipy middle schoolers, but you'd be wrong.

We pull up in front of the apartment building and Haley's breath hitches. "What—oh my God. What is he doing here!?"

I frown and follow her gaze to see a man with a ton of piercings wearing worn black jeans with holes in them and a ratty band shirt leaning against a motorcycle, parked in front of the building. I park behind him and Haley gets out of the car like her ass is on fire.

"Reed, what the hell are you doing here!?"

The guy, Reed, lights up when he sees her. "Haley, baby, c'mon, we gotta talk."

"No, no, there is nothing to talk about." Haley folds her arms and keeps six feet of distance from him. "We already said everything we needed to say. And did everything we needed to do."

"I'm sorry, okay? I'm sorry. It was a mistake—"

"Eating my leftovers is a mistake! Forgetting to get gas is a mistake! Cheating on me is a *choice*."

Oh, I see how it is. I get out of the car and walk up. "What's going on here?"

Haley and Reed both glare at me, but she gestures at Reed. "Reed, meet my boss. Boss? Meet my ex-boyfriend."

Oh boy.

Chapter 5

Haley

When we pull up in front of the apartment and I see none other than Reed with his motorcycle in front of the building, I almost can't breathe. I don't want to deal with this. I don't want to deal with *him*.

The guy went and broke my heart. He cheated on me with several women. And now he shows up after I moved to a whole new city? What the hell could he possibly want from me?

He doesn't look great. He's in the clothes that he tends to wear when he's depressed. *Good,* I think viciously. *You should be depressed since you lost me. I was the best goddamn thing that ever happened to you.*

Even as I think it, I'm not sure that I believe it. I've had nothing but bad boyfriends all my adult life. After a while you have to look at the common denominator, right?

But that doesn't mean that I'm going to sit here and let Reed try and win me back. Maybe I'm part of the problem, but I'm not going to be treated like crap anymore. Not by my boss and not by my ex-boyfriend.

Although, I have to admit, when I tell Jack who Reed is,

I can't help but notice the difference between them. Jack walks up to ask what's going on, wearing his sleek bespoke blue suit, one that brings out the color in his eyes, a bit of five o'clock shadow and his loosened tie making him look ever-so-slightly rakish.

He looks confident, successful, and put together. Nothing at all like Reed, who looks like a damn mess. My ex-boyfriend doesn't look like the sexy bad boy who sweet-talked me into a relationship. He looks like... well, honestly, he looks like a loser.

Jack glances between Reed and me. "Is this a stalking case? Do I need to call the police?"

"What?" Reed splutters. "What the fuck? Back off, this isn't your problem."

"Haley works for me. That does, in fact, make it my problem. And when someone is being harassed and stalked, then I think it's *everyone's* problem." Jack steps forward, putting himself between Reed and me. "Do I need to make you clear off?"

"He's not stalking me," I tell him, because even though I love the idea of Reed being embarrassed, I don't want this to become a bigger mess than it already is. I don't want any fuss, I just want my cheating ex out of my life. "Although I would love to know where the hell you get the audacity to think that you can show up here and win me back."

"Haley, c'mon." Reed flashes me that grin of his, the one that used to make my knees go weak. I'd swoon over that grin. Now, it just makes my stomach queasy. "You know that you miss me. Remember how good things used to be between us? We can have that again! I ruined a great thing, I get that now, but I miss you. My apartment's so lonely and empty without you."

"You mean it's dirty without her to clean up after you," Jack says, his tone mild.

I nearly burst out into laughter and just barely choke it back in time. "Reed, I'm not taking you back. You treated me like trash."

Reed tries to come towards me. "Haley—"

Jack takes a step to the side so he remains in between us. "Where are you from?"

The question surprises Reed so much he answers automatically. "Portland."

"So you had to come here from Portland."

Reed shrugs. "Anything for love, y'know?"

"No," Jack corrects him. "It means that Haley moved from Portland all the way to a new city." He looks at me. "Is that right?"

I nod.

"Now, last I checked—I don't have your resume memorized, Haley, but I remember it being impressive. Is there a shortage of parents who need nannies in Portland, Haley? Did you have to move here to address a nanny shortage?"

I shake my head.

"So you could've stayed in Portland if you wanted."

I nod.

Jack turns back to face Reed. "So what I'm understanding is that this woman moves to a whole other city to get away from you after you cheat on her—"

"Multiple times," I add.

"Wow." Jack's brows rise. "Several times? And you decided to chase her down to a new city? And you're claiming that's romantic? Did you bring roses? A damn mixtape? *Anything* romantic as a gift to show your commitment?"

It's pretty damn clear he didn't.

"And are you in therapy?" Jack adds. "Have you done anything that will prove to her that you're not lying to her now? That you'll hold to your commitment to be loyal to her?"

Reed opens his mouth, then closes it. He glares. "I ought to teach you a damn lesson to keep your nose out of other people's business, asshole. This is between Haley and me, not anybody else. Unless you're also fucking her and you're mad I'm taking away your free ride."

Jack moves so fast I don't even see it.

Reed yells and stumbles back, his hands on his face. "You broke my nose!" he yells.

Jack shakes out his hand, wincing a little. "Damn. Been a while since I punched someone."

"You punch people regularly?" I ask weakly.

"Not anymore. You should've seen me in college. I painted the town red." Jack glares at Reed. "Your girlfriend stayed loyal to you and you want to insinuate she's fucking her boss? What the fuck is wrong with you? You don't fucking respect her. And Haley, I know for a fact, is someone who deserves a hell of a lot of respect. So you get on that piece of shit you're daring to call a motorcycle, and you're going to take your poser ass back to Portland, and you're going to leave Haley the fuck alone. Or I will expend my considerable resources into making your life a living hell. Are we clear?"

Reed glares at him, but I see fear in his eyes now. The knot in my stomach loosens a little.

After a moment more of glaring, Reed flips Jack off and gets onto his bike. "Call me when you change your mind," he calls to me. "And you realize I was the best damn thing you ever had."

He pulls away from the curb and drives off.

My knees wobble a little. Instantly Jack's hands are on my shoulders, guiding me to lean against the car. "Hey, there, easy now."

He tilts my chin up so he can look me in the eyes. My breath catches in my throat. He just looks so concerned, so earnest, and his hands on me are strong and protective.

This is the man who helped a random woman when she was about to slip and hurt herself in a bar. This was the guy who helped clean me up and gave me his jacket so that I wouldn't be uncomfortable on the picnic bench while we had sex.

Jack's arm slides around me a little more, and I find myself pressing in, my fingers seizing on the lapels of his ten-thousand-dollar suit.

"A firecracker like you deserves so much better than that weasel," he murmurs, his gaze dropping down to my mouth.

"I know now," I whisper. "You showed me how."

Blame it on the adrenaline, blame it on wanting to get the bad taste of seeing Reed again out of my mouth, but either way, I'm not thinking straight at all; and before I know what I'm doing, I'm pressing my mouth to his.

Jack kisses me back instantly, his fingers tightening on my chin to hold me in place as his tongue slides into my mouth. He kisses just as good as I remember, and I feel like my body is molding itself to his, pressing us together in every way possible.

I need to breathe and start to pull away—and Jack wrenches his mouth back. "Sorry."

"Sorry? I'm the one who kissed you."

"And I'm your boss." Jack pushes me gently back against the car, his hands on my shoulders. "We can't—I'm sorry."

"No, no, I'm sorry. I don't know what came over me." I know it's wrong and would for sure ruin Jack's reputation—I can see the tabloid headlines now—but that doesn't change how much I want to kiss him again and invite him upstairs.

"Adrenaline is a hell of a drug," Jack replies. His thumbs stroke back and forth over my shoulders, like he can't help himself. I should remove his hands. I don't. "Do I need to call the police? Did he ever hurt you? Do you need to take out a restraining order?"

I shake my head. Reed was a total asshole when he was drunk, and sometimes when he was sober, but he never hit me. "No. No, it's fine. I just—I just didn't think I'd ever see him again."

"I get it. It's a lot." Jack rubs my back. "Just breathe. A person doesn't have to physically hurt you to make you a bit panicked when you see them again."

I nod and wipe at my eyes, realizing they're wet. "Yeah. He's just. A real piece of shit."

"Any guy who cheats is a real piece of shit, but especially someone who cheats over and over. You're too good for him."

I roll my eyes. "Yeah, right. Don't lie to me."

"What? I'm not lying."

"Oh, yeah? Then why'd you go from charming to an asshole to me the moment you finished getting your rocks off with me?"

Jack frowns. "You were about to ask me for my number. I promise you it's not personal, but I don't do that. I don't do serious relationships, just sex. I've learned that even if I tell a woman this, they don't always believe me and I end up just breaking their hearts. So now I'm a... a one-night-only type of guy."

I appreciate his attempt at humor, but I'm still too busy

being annoyed with him to laugh. "You thought I—I wasn't going to ask for your number. Your bandmate came up. I was going to ask for your CD or demo, and ask about your band. You were one of the bar performers."

Jack's face pales, then flushes with embarrassment. "...oh."

"Yeah, *oh*." I shake my head. "I'm not doing relationships anymore. Well. Not right now. I want one. I've always wanted to be a mother, and I want a partner for that, but—"

"Reed." Jack nods. "I get it, that kind of thing takes time to get over."

"Yeah, but it's not even just Reed. He was just the latest. I have a thing for"—I do quotation marks in the air—"bad boys."

"Ah." The corner of Jack's mouth quirks up. "I bet my leather jacket really did it for you then, huh?"

"Sure did."

"Is this a bad time to tell you about my tattoos?"

I groan and manage to laugh this time. "Very funny."

"I really do have tattoos." Jack sobers up. "The problem with 'bad boys' is that it's hard to tell who's just rough around the edges and—"

"And who's an actual piece of shit? Yeah. I seem to attract a lot of that kind." I shrug. "So I swore off dating for a while. I'm not going to be treated like that again."

"You shouldn't be," Jack promises me. "You deserve better. I meant it when I said that."

I can't help the shock I feel, and I'm sure it's written all over my face. Jack winces and steps back, his hands falling away from me. I'm surprised at how disappointed I am that he's no longer touching me.

"You really respect me that much?" I blurt out. "I

47

thought that you were convinced I was... I thought you didn't like me because we slept together."

"Really?" Jack looks as shocked as I feel. "Haley, I don't dislike you at all. I think that you're an excellent nanny. I just didn't want you to have any kind of false impression about our relationship, and especially now that you're my employee I wanted to keep a distance."

I fold my arms. "Well. Thank you. I appreciate it."

"Of course. You were...." Jack clears his throat, his eyes a little dark. "You were great. I had a great time with you. I'm just not the kind of man who will ever get into a relationship again. And as my employee—"

"Oh God no, no." I nod in agreement. "Right, no I agree. It would be wildly inappropriate for us to do anything and I wasn't expecting that at all. My commitment is to Penny and to doing this job well."

"Thank you. I'm sorry that I gave you the impression I didn't... I would never disrespect someone for having a healthy sex life outside of work. It's none of my business."

I nod, a bit overwhelmed by all of this.

"I understand the bad-boy appeal," Jack adds quietly. He smirks. "I got a lot of girls with that image. And the whole reason that I got tattoos, started dressing that way, got a motorcycle, was because I saw other men like that and I thought they were cool. I wanted to be like them. So I really do get it. But you deserve to wait for someone who will treat you right."

"Thank you," I tell him, and I mean it. "For defending me back there, and for giving me a ride, and paying for the tow truck... I don't think I thanked you for those, either, yet, so. Thank you."

"Anytime, Haley, and I mean it." His thumb strokes my chin, and my breath catches in my throat. All in a rush, I remember what it was like to have his hands on me, his tongue in my mouth, his—

Jack clears his throat and steps back. "You good to go up to your apartment?"

I nod.

Jack smiles. It's so warm and attractive, and I finally can see the charming man who swept me off my feet at the bar. Fuck, he really is attractive. "I'll let you go, then. Have a good night, Haley."

He walks around me and gets back into his car. I push away and head up towards my apartment, not letting myself look back as he drives away.

"Hey," Sara calls from the couch as I enter. "You're late, I was just about to call you and make sure you were okay. Everything good?"

There are a lot of ways to answer that question, but in spite of everything with my car and with my ex, the biggest concern in my mind is my boss.

I don't know how to feel about him now, and what's worse, I'm still attracted to him.

This has the potential to be a big mess.

Chapter 6

Jack

Fucking hell, I've been an asshole.

I jumped the gun and assumed Haley wanted my number, and all she wanted was to ask me about my band and get a demo. She wanted to be *supportive*. The bar we went to has a lot of indie bands and people who are just starting out and trying to get their name out there, and while most of those artists are younger, some of them are middle-aged like I am.

She was trying to be a good audience member and support someone she thought was an indie artist, and I shut her down and walked away.

Fuck.

It's really a pity that she's my employee, because hearing that she's taking a major break from relationships, and knowing how good it felt to fuck her... under any other circumstances I'd be telling her we should do something casual.

Haley's blunt, that's for sure. She has no problem telling me what she thinks and pushing my buttons if it'll get her the result she wants. If I told her that I just wanted sex, I think I could actually trust her, because she's looking just for sex too.

And who the fuck can blame her, after what that asshole did to her. She told me that Reed was just the latest, but I saw her face when she was talking to him. If he was just the most recent boyfriend to cause that heartbroken, betrayed look on her face, then I can't even imagine how raw and wounded she feels inside.

It's infuriating. Haley's a good person and she deserves so much better. That weasel thinks he's so tough, so badass, but a man who knows just how badass he is doesn't need to flaunt it. And he definitely doesn't treat the people around him like crap. Especially not someone he claims to love.

It takes actual strength to be a community leader. To forge new paths. To treat everyone with respect and kindness. You beat up a sucker because he was mouthing off to a woman or being a shithead, not just because you think it makes you some kind of alpha male. Real alphas, real wolves, take care of their damn packs.

Reed is just another poser who probably doesn't even fix up his motorcycle himself. That piece of crap wouldn't stand a chance if he was trying to roll with an actual motorcycle gang. He's the kind of fake "bad boy" who just talks the talk and looks enough of the part to get laid.

Disgusting.

I didn't come from money. Neither did my bandmates. Mark grew up in the city in a bad part of town, but the rest of us were out in the middle of nowhere. I'm ninety percent sure the bar I snuck out to as a teenager didn't even have a liquor license. They sure never carded me, even though I know I didn't look twenty-one.

Reed wouldn't have stood a chance in that place, or any

of the places that my bandmates and I come from. I know that for a fact.

The sheer audacity makes my blood boil. He didn't warn her he was coming. He just showed up. I saw the look on her face when she realized it was him.

Now, I believe Haley when she says he never hit her. But when someone cheats on you and ruins your trust like that, seeing them with no warning? That has to be upsetting. Possibly even anxiety-inducing.

Not only did he not give her any kind of damn warning, he didn't even bother to give her a gift? Something heartfelt? I'm not expecting someone to break their back on a diamond necklace or something trite like that, but he should've brought something. Something thoughtful, something that would remind her of something important in their relationship... perhaps her favorite flowers, or some baked goods from a favorite place in Portland. Fuck, get her a damn gift card to her favorite clothing store. Not to buy Haley's forgiveness, but to show that he paid attention to her. That he really does care about her.

But Reed did nothing. He just showed up, cocky and full of the assumption that if he just told her he was sorry and looked a bit pathetic, she'd take him back. I bet his apartment stinks right now and he's realized just how much Haley used to take care of him.

"Bad boys" like that aren't really "bad boys." They're just whiny children who use their persona to get away with being lazy. Haley probably had to do so much work to keep the place clean, to put food on the table, to make meals, like she was his damn mother.

If that guy shows up anywhere near her again, I'm going to make sure he stays away permanently. I think he learned his lesson, though.

My knuckles ache as I grip the steering wheel, but I don't regret punching him. I'll just put my hand on ice when I get home. The shit deserved more than just one punch for cheating on Haley multiple times.

I've got to fix things between Haley and myself. I was such a jerk to her at the bar and that's got to be why she's so angry at me all the time. And who can blame her? I need to fix this and repair our relationship, make up for my mistake and show her that I respect her.

But first...

"Call Mark," I say to my car system.

Mark picks up on the second ring. "Hey, you free this weekend?"

"Next time, could you not mention that I'm a bassist in front of someone?" I ask him.

"What are you talking about?"

"That girl I had with me at the bar a month ago, you were talking about my music in front of her. She wanted a demo of our stuff."

"Why, is she a music producer?"

"No, she was just trying to be supportive."

"And you're squeamish about this a whole month later. It still bothering you that much? I don't remember her asking for our music, you cut her off before she could say anything." I can hear the smile in Mark's voice. Oh boy. "Unless you're still talking to her."

"No..."

"You are, aren't you? She just asked for our music again and you're still talking to her. A whole month, JJ, wow—"

"Mark." JJ is the name I went by starting freshman year because there were, for some reason, three other Jacks in my year. Joseph is my middle name, so I started going by JJ. I stopped after college when I had to be professional, but my bandmates still use it. "It's not what you think."

"I think that you might finally be ready to move on from Emily, is what I think."

"For crying out loud. Forget I even called you." I hang up on him.

I'm not moving on from Emily. Emily was the love of my life, the woman I was supposed to be with, and she was taken from me. Nobody else is going to replace her, and I'm not going to break my heart and someone else's by trying.

End of story.

Chapter 7

Haley

I t's the weirdest thing. Ever since the run-in with Reed and my car trouble, Jack's started to be... *nice* to me.

I have no idea what to do about this.

For one thing, it's weird to go from arguing all the time and sending each other passive-aggressive notes to getting along. I actually kind of miss him doing things like buying new locks for his office, so I can pick them and sneak more of Penny's assignments onto his desk.

For another, Jack being nice to me is actually... a problem. A worse problem than when he was rude to me. I almost wish he'd go back to being rude, because when he was rude, I could ignore how hot he is.

Now he's being nice and it's all I can think about.

I've never been so well treated by a man before, and I'm finding that being treated with such consideration and thoughtfulness is... really, really attractive.

Jack asks how my day is going.

He asks me to make a list of my favorite foods so that they'll be in the kitchen for me.

He pays to fix up my car and pays to have a driver take

me to and from his house until it's fixed and I can drive again.

Before, I would save receipts every time I spent money for Penny, like museum tickets, and I would send the receipts to Deborah so that she could reimburse me. But now, Jack's given me a credit card with no limit and told me to use it for Penny however I want. He even told me to use it to order in food for myself or little things like that.

"Just don't take it and run away to France for a spa week and a shopping spree," he tells me with a grin, "and you'll be fine."

I'm tempted to do just that, if only because he'll be angry with me and we'll be back on familiar ground.

I can only assume that this is how Jack treated the last nanny as well, and he was damn lucky she was happily married. I could see any employee feeling special with this treatment. I hope this isn't how he treated the women he was trying to have casual, just-sex relationships with, otherwise I'm completely on their side as to why they wanted more.

How are you supposed to do anything except get a crush on someone when they treat you like this?

It's maddening. And on top of all of that, he's handsome as sin.

Every morning I have to deal with Jack leaving right as I arrive for the day, and every morning, he's dressed to the nines. It's clear that he's a man who actually understands suit quality and cut, and picks his own fabrics or at the very least has a strong sense of personal style and asks his stylist to follow a guideline.

He never dresses in just a boring suit, or an ill-fitting suit, or black. Instead, he favors dark muted colors with a little pop of a brighter color in a tie or pocket square. Sometimes the fabric of the suit will have a subtle pattern on it, the kind you need to pay attention to pick out, but even if you just glance at him casually, the pattern lends depth to the whole look.

Jack looks like a billionaire. No, more than that. He looks like a man on top of the world, a man who owns everything, and it's unbearably sexy.

Something that's always drawn me to bad boys is how they act like they're the sexiest, biggest, baddest wolves in the forest. Jack has that exact same attitude, just like he's bringing it to the boardroom rather than a bar. It makes my mouth go dry and my stomach go hot.

When he was being an asshole to me, I could ignore all of this. We barely saw each other in person. He'd leave as I arrived and he'd ignore me, and I'd roll my eyes and ignore him. Then he'd come home late, after Penny was asleep, and I'd leave and we'd barely exchange a word to each other.

Now he wants to chat with me in the morning, and in the evening, and I have to look at his stupid, handsome face and listen to his stupid, sexy voice and pretend that I'm not attracted to him because he's my boss.

Sometimes I wonder if the universe is laughing at me. I swear off men, and so the universe gives me a fantastic guy, the kind of guy I'd love to date or at the least have some regular amazing sex with... and he's off-limits.

Ugh.

I try to keep it under wraps and to keep it professional. I don't let myself get flirtatious and I try to keep snarks to a minimum. It's hard, though; because I could be wrong, but Jack seems to... like it, when I'm sassy?

I remember Deborah telling me that he didn't fire me for fighting with him immediately because he's used to a bunch of "yes men" around him and she liked that I stood up for myself and wasn't cowed. But surely a guy like Jack doesn't like it when his nanny is breaking into his home office and fighting with him at every turn.

I just need to keep my head down and focus on Penny.

Or... maybe....

Maybe this is the opening I need.

Jack refuses to spend any time with his daughter. They do spend *some* time together, they have to, living in the same house; but it's about as much time as I spent with Sara when she was my roommate in college and we worked different times and none of our classes lined up. That semester was hard. I only really saw her when she was taking a nap, or briefly while one of us was coming or going.

That's one thing with your roommate for a semester. It's another thing entirely when it's your parent.

I don't know why Jack refuses to be a father to Penny, but it's unacceptable. If he didn't want to be a parent then why have the kid in the first place? He and whoever Penny's mom was could've given Penny up for adoption when she was born. It would've been better for her, if you ask me, to be adopted by parents who eagerly hoped for a child and applied to be parents, rather than stuck with a man who shows her every day that she's not a priority.

She might only be five, but kids can feel that kind of thing, even if they're not yet old enough to articulate it. And Penny's such a good, adorable kid. She's creative and loves drawing and playing dinosaurs in the backyard. Every day that I pick her up from kindergarten she spends the entire car ride telling me all about her friends, the things she learned, and the fun arts and crafts they did.

She's a whole human being, vibrant and joyful. I don't

understand how Jack could be her father and not want to be a part of that.

I wait until the end of the day when Jack comes home from work and Penny's already in bed. I know that Jack works his ass off and he's probably tired, but the only other option is in the morning when he's on his way out the door and I don't want to make him late for work or risk Penny overhearing.

I wait for him in the foyer. He's wearing a dark green suit today with a very subtle stripe pattern and a soft, forest green tie. It contrasts wonderfully with his eyes. It's the end of the day, so he's loosened the tie and undone a couple buttons on his shirt, his hair curling and floppy from running his hands through it, and fuck, I want him to do so many sinful things to me.

"Hey." Jack smiles, looking a little surprised. "You have somewhere to be?"

"No."

"Oh, looked like you were waiting for me, I figured you were off somewhere. It is a Friday. You could be off to a concert or something."

"You wildly overestimate my social life."

"Well, you said it yourself, you're into bad boys." He undoes his tie completely and takes off his jacket, rolling up the sleeves of his shirt to expose his forearms. I don't whimper, but it's a close thing. Fuck, he really had to look like a cover model, huh?

Honestly, the age difference and the touch of silver in his hair doesn't deter me. In a way it actually... makes him hotter.

"In my experience," Jack goes on, "if you're looking for bad boys, you go to where they hang out. And you're also usually into the same things they are like loud concerts, dive bars, motorcycle rallies—"

"That was me in high school and college," I point out. "I'm older now."

"You're not even thirty."

"Never too young to start being mature!"

Jack shakes his head. "I dropped all of that fun stuff to start my company, right out of college. Trust me, you're going to miss the choice to be young and crazy for a little while longer."

"You regret it?"

"Not exactly." Jack clears his throat, and I can tell he's uncomfortable with the conversation.

"Besides," I add instead, trying to lighten the mood before I bring down the hammer, "I told you I was swearing off bad boys, remember? Why would I go to where the bad boys are if I'm trying to avoid temptation?"

"Very fair point."

"But I was waiting for you," I add, before my courage can fail me.

Jack looks delighted. "Oh?"

I take a deep breath and force my voice to stay light and calm. It's possible that I started out way too strong before because I didn't like Jack and I thought he didn't like me. I had nothing to lose. But now he's being nice to me and seems to genuinely respect me, and I don't want to ruin that.

"Since we're getting along so well now that our whole misunderstanding's been cleared up," I start, "I was wondering if this weekend you'd like to join Penny and me—"

"No," Jack cuts me off before I can even finish the sentence.

"Just like that, huh?" I keep my voice soft.

"Just like that," Jack affirms. That cold attitude is back, the one I hate. "I made myself clear when I hired you, and I've been reiterating that ever since. If you can't seem to get it through your head, that's not my problem. I thought you'd understood."

"And I thought that maybe I could get through to you now that you weren't stonewalling me."

"Did you think that my refusal to see my daughter had to do with you?" Jack snorts. "Don't flatter yourself."

"I thought that it was you being your jackass self," I shoot back. "But I had hoped that now we're on better terms you might actually listen to me and I could change your mind."

"You can't change my mind. If it was possible to sway me on this, don't you think that someone in the last five years would've managed it?"

"No," I say, bluntly. "Because everyone else is afraid of you. Even Deborah doesn't stand up to you as much as she should, because she's paid to be your assistant, not your conscience. She does what you tell her. But I'm not paid to follow your orders, I'm paid to look after your daughter. The daughter that, apparently, you don't even want."

"Careful," Jack growls, and oh fuck that voice should not be nearly so hot as it is to me. Heat shivers through me and I wonder how this would feel if he wasn't angry with me over something so serious, if I was just pushing back for the sake of pushing, and he got stern with me like that and put me over his knee...

"You're starting to get into things that aren't any of your business," Jack finishes, and I snap back to reality. Fuck, stop it, I can't have inappropriate fantasies about my boss

61

like this. Especially not when I'm trying to push him on something so important.

"I'm Penny's nanny. That makes it my business. Jack, she's so lovely. If you just spent an hour or two with her you'd see it. You'll love her, I just know it—"

"I don't care if she's lovely, or if she's the most spoiled brat this side of Veruca Salt," Jack snaps. "I run my household and my family the way I want to, and while you don't have to like it, you *do* have to obey."

"My God," I snap, my mouth running away with me before I can stop myself, "you must've really hated your wife to treat her daughter like this."

Jack's mouth drops open in shock and I realize what I've just said. My hand flies to my mouth in horror, but it's too late to stop the words.

I grab my purse and flee out the front door before I can make things even worse.

Chapter 8

Jack

I don't know what I was hoping for when I saw that Haley had been in the foyer waiting for me, but it sure as hell wasn't this.

Haley is my employee. I keep repeating that to myself, over and over, but it's hard to tell my damn body that.

I'm glad that she seems to be keeping things professional. I can still feel her mouth against mine from when she kissed me against my car after Reed showed up. The desperation in her body and the way that she moved... how she felt against me...

I'd been so close to opening the car door and shoving her in to take her right there, to remind her what a real man fucked like, to show her for once and for all that I can give her what that pathetic excuse for her ex never could even dream of giving her.

It was probably just adrenaline on her part. Even if she wasn't my employee, I'm glad we didn't go further that time. She'd just had a bad shock and that isn't a good headspace to make decisions like who you're going to sleep with.

And given how professional she's been with me since, I

think I can safely say she doesn't have any interest in me. I am, after all, the very kind of guy she said she was swearing off.

And yet my gut had done this weird stupid flutter when I saw her waiting for me, and when she confirmed that's what she'd been doing.

Then she dropped that damn bombshell.

I was so damn angry with her. I give very simple instructions and she can't adhere to them? If she has such a problem with how I want my relationship with my daughter to be, then she should just quit. But then she says *that*.

"My god, you must've really hated your wife to treat her daughter like this."

It stops me dead in my tracks.

And the thing is... she's right.

She's not right in that I didn't love my wife. I loved Emily very much. So much, so that when she died, I couldn't bear to be around our daughter.

Penelope was a reminder of everything that I'd lost. She looks so much like her mother. I instantly saw Emily's eyes in our baby, and the older Penelope got, the more and more she looked like the woman I'd lost. It had hurt me to see her, and so I kept her away. I still keep her away.

But when Haley says those words, they hit me right in the chest like she'd stabbed me in the heart with a needle.

After she runs out the door, I know I should go after her, but I can't. I just stand there, rooted to the spot, staring at the spot where Haley just stood.

Because she's right.

Emily and I were so excited to have a child together. We'd talked about parenthood as the symbol of our recommitment to each other. The pregnancy had been difficult for

Emily almost from the beginning, but she'd been so excited to be a mother. I'd been excited to be a father.

Then everything went wrong with the labor, and while our daughter made it out, Emily didn't.

Emily would hate what I've done with Penelope. Our beloved daughter arrived and I've neglected her. Emily would be furious with me. She'd berate me, and rightly so.

Emily wasn't much like Haley. She was flighty whereas Haley's committed; creative whereas Haley is grounded; and quiet and insecure whereas Haley is loud and stubborn. But I think she'd have no problem telling me off, just like Haley, in this particular instance.

I have to sit down and contemplate everything, gathering my thoughts and restructuring them. All this time, I've been failing the woman I loved; the very reason that I avoided our daughter in the first place.

Eventually, when I can get my legs to work, I go up to Penelope's room.

I expect her to be asleep, but when I slip into the room, I see that there's a tent under the covers and the telltale glow of a flashlight. I smile.

"You know, I used to do the same thing when I was your age," I whisper, pulling the covers back.

Penelope jolts in surprise and slams shut the picture book she was reading, trying in vain to hide it and the flashlight. I chuckle. "I love how much you love reading, but you should be asleep right now."

"Sorry, Daddy." Her eyes are wide as she watches me put away the book and the flashlight. "What are you doing?"

"I wanted to check on you."

"While I was sleeping?"

"Uh-huh. I just wanted to see you. Make sure you were okay."

Penelope chews on her lip. "Do you do that? A lot?"

I swallow. I want to tell her *yes*, to give her a happy lie, but I don't want to set a precedent of lying to my daughter when I've just made the decision to start a proper relationship with her.

"No," I say honestly. "I don't. I've never done this before."

I sit down on the edge of her bed. "I talked with Haley. She loves you a lot."

Penelope nods. "I love her a lot."

"Good, I'm glad. I don't want you to have a nanny you don't love. But Haley told me that I was being a bad daddy to you because I wouldn't spend time with you. And I didn't want to listen to her. But she's very stubborn, and she finally convinced me that she was right."

I pass my hand through my daughter's curls, curls that are just like her mother's were. "I haven't been there for you, sweetheart, and I'm really sorry about that. Do you think you could give me a chance to do it right?"

I fully expect her to feel uncomfortable and awkward. She doesn't owe me a damn thing, honestly. Her entire young life, I've ignored her or been cold. What reason does she have to feel affection or trust towards me?

Hell, she probably even resents me.

But instead, Penelope gives me a wide smile. "You mean you'll play dinosaurs with me? And make me pancakes?"

"I sure do. Are those specific requests?"

Penelope nods, her curls bouncing. "Haley says those are things daddies do with their kids."

"Haley is very smart. Don't tell her I told you this, but I think she might be smarter than I am."

Penelope giggles, her hands over her mouth. I smile at her, my heart swelling.

She's a lot like Emily. Of course, she is. But she's not actually my late wife. She's her own person. Especially now that she's five, she's got her own personality for sure. And I've been missing out on it by acting like she's the ghost of someone else.

"We can't do any of those things, though, if you don't go to sleep," I warn her.

Penelope lies down in bed and pulls the covers up to her chin. "Okay."

I start to get up to leave, but her small hand grabs mine. "Daddy, will you stay a little bit?"

I sit back down. "Of course I can." It's the least of what I owe her.

Penelope smiles and closes her eyes, but occasionally she peeks one open again, just to make sure I'm still there. I get myself settled alongside her in bed so that she can see me, and eventually, her eyes stop peeking open, and her breaths become deep and even.

I should go and get ready for bed myself, but I can't stop watching her.

I remember at the hospital when she was put into my arms, right after the doctor told me that they were unable to stop Emily's bleeding. The most wonderful moment of my life had turned into the most tragic, and then I had this tiny creature in my arms, and somehow, I was supposed to ignore my own grief and take care of her.

That was something I hadn't known how to do. I'd been forty at the time, and you'd think that being that age would make me somewhat mature enough to handle this, but I hadn't been, not at all. I had seriously floundered.

Now I'd had my wake-up call, and my chance to make it

right, and I can't stop staring at her. It was like all the wonder I was supposed to feel at Penelope's birth is hitting me now, and all I can do is let it wash over me like a wave.

I don't even mean to do it, but at some point between one blink and the next, I fall asleep.

Chapter 9

Haley

I really hope I can avoid Jack when I come in for work this morning.

I still can't believe I said that to him. I should apologize, but after working on an apology text for hours last night, I realized that it would be trite of me to do it over text, and I should probably give him a chance to cool down anyway, so in person would be better.

But now I'm pulling up the drive and I really don't want to have to see him at all, even if an apology is the right thing to do. I just want a hole to swallow me up.

Honestly, I wasn't even sure if I should come to work today. Jack's probably going to fire me the second he sees me. But I can't leave Penny in the lurch. It'll be at least a few days before Jack finds a replacement for me, and in the meantime, I'm not going to disappear on her with no warning.

Jack's car is still in the driveway when I pull up. Damn it. I had even left the apartment a few minutes late hoping he'd have already left for work when I got here, but no such luck.

I park and head inside, but to my surprise, Jack isn't waiting for me.

There's no sign of him in the kitchen. The coffee machine has made a fresh pot, but that doesn't mean much. It's one of those fancy machines that can make espressos and cappuccinos. You put a whole bag of coffee in it and set an alarm, and it automatically brews however many cups of coffee you programmed it to make at the same time every morning.

I go to Jack's office, but the door's open and he's not inside.

Huh. Must be in his wing of the house, I guess. It's so ridiculous to me that he has his own end of the house upstairs separate from his daughter's. I've said so before.

I've really been so pushy with him when it comes to the Penny issue. I should've been more patient, and gentler. I should've trod with more care.

Too late now.

Might as well go upstairs to wake up Penelope. It's Saturday, which doesn't seem to make a difference to Jack as far as work goes, he heads out in the morning anyway, either to the golf course (I still find it amusing that he hates that) or somewhere else to schmooze, or wine and dine, or do some charity thing or other. One thing nobody can accuse Jack Steele of is being miserly with his money.

But for Penny, it means that she doesn't have to go to kindergarten, so I can let her sleep in a little. I'll make pancakes or something else a bit special for her since it's the weekend...

I tiptoe upstairs and open the door to check on her, and nearly fall over in shock.

Jack.

Jack is in Penny's bed, curled up around her in an

awkward position. One of his legs is falling off the bed—he even still has all of his clothes on, including his shoes.

It's clear he didn't mean to fall asleep like this, and I have to stifle a giggle at how adorable he looks. I wish I could see more of this Jack, unguarded and rumpled.

But what the hell is he doing in his daughter's room? He never comes here.

I tiptoe over and gently shake him awake. "Jack," I whisper, keeping my voice as soft as possible so that Penny won't wake up.

She's turned towards her father, her little face completely at peace, like she fell asleep looking at him. It's so sweet it makes my heart want to burst.

Jack blinks slowly, his gaze cloudy and confused. He turns towards me, squinting a little, and he looks so handsome and disheveled that I can barely hold myself in check. I want to kiss him so badly it hurts. I want to see him wake up like this after a night of debauchery together.

Damn it, this is getting dangerously close to a crush.

Jack looks at me in confusion. "Haley?" he whispers.

"You're in Penny's bed," I whisper back.

Jack looks confused for another second, and then his face clears up. "Ah."

He pushes himself up and winces. "I must've fallen asleep here by accident." He gestures toward the door, and I head out, Jack following behind me and then gently closing the door after us.

"What were you doing?" I ask, the both of us walking down the hallway so that we won't disturb Penny. "You need a shower. What the hell?"

"Wow, thanks, polite way of telling me I stink."

"You smell go—fine." I correct myself from saying *good*

just in time. "But you slept in last night's clothes. A shower will do you wonders."

"Whatever the doctor orders."

I can hear the snark in his tone, and I brace myself and stop walking. "Mr. Steele."

"Jack."

"Jack." I make myself look him in the eye. "I'm so sorry about what I said last night. It was inappropriate, and it crossed a line. I shouldn't have said it, and I understand if you want to give me my two weeks' notice because of it."

He stares at me for a second. "Why are—you don't need to apologize."

I blink a few times in surprise. "What are you talking about? Of course I need to apologize. What I said was completely out of line."

Jack winces. "Maybe it was, maybe it wasn't, but whether or not it was inappropriate for my employee to tell me that... for *anyone* to tell me that... you were right. I needed to hear it."

Now I'm the one staring. "Are you—you're serious?"

I don't think he would joke about something like this, but I want to double-check. I need to double-check, to make sure I'm not about to be fired.

Jack chuckles a little at the expression on my face. "Yes, I'm serious. I've appreciated from the beginning how dedicated you are to my daughter. It's what I expect in a nanny. She needs a father and I... I need to respect the memory of my wife better."

Oh, wow, he really is serious. "I'm really glad to hear it, Mr.—Jack. I really am. Penny would love to spend more time with you. She asks about you all the time."

Jack sighs. "I had thought she might resent me. Five years, especially the first five years of a child's life... that's a lot of time for her to grow accustomed to thinking that I don't care about her."

"Well, I'm glad that she doesn't resent you. I don't think she could. She's too sweet for that. She's a really lovely girl, seriously, you're lucky to have her."

"Well, it's not because of me that she's like that." Jack turns and heads into his wing of the house, and for a second I think the conversation's over, but then he glances over his shoulder at me, and I realize he's just doing that thing, where he does his own thing and expects everyone to just follow along with him.

I roll my eyes, hating the fond warmth in my chest. Jack is still Jack Steele, agreeing with me about his daughter or not, and that means he's still a commanding man used to everyone following his orders even when they're unspoken.

I follow him down the hall. I've never been into this part of the house, never had a reason to be here. It's done up in the same décor as the rest of the house, lovely greens and browns with small pops of color to imitate a forest, but with a more mature and elegant design, like something out of an old mansion.

"You're a bit old-fashioned," I note.

"It wasn't really my style," Jack replies. "I built this place for my wife."

"You built this place?"

"Yes. I'm much more... rock n' roll." He grins at me, but then the smile fades from his face. "I loved her a lot... Emily."

"Penelope's mother."

"Yes." Jack opens the door to his bedroom. "I wanted this house to be her dream home."

I can feel my eyes going wide as he leads me into a luxurious master bedroom, complete with a four-poster bed that looks like it's been carved out of one large piece of wood, styled to look like a huge tree. "Wow."

"You like it?"

"It's not my style. I'm more rock n' roll." I grin at him. "But I can appreciate it. It's beautiful. Honestly, I'm glad you did this place up like this because Penny adores it. She loves pretending to be a dinosaur in the forest or a lost fairy, things like that."

Jack nods thoughtfully. "Good to know."

"Let's get you into the shower." I head through the bedroom into a large bathroom that stops me in my tracks. "Holy shit."

"Y'know, it's amusing how impressed you are."

I turn to see Jack grinning at me. I glare at him. "Well, you might've been able to get used to it, Mr. Billionaire, but some of us still share a bathroom with our roommate."

I walk through the beautifully tiled room, up to the large rain shower, and turn it on. "Now get in and clean yourself up. I'm going to make breakfast."

"I'm sorry, who's the boss around here?" Jack obligingly starts taking off his shirt even as he teases me.

I force myself to look away before I do something stupid like beg to see his tattoos. Now that I know he has them, I want to see them, and I didn't get to see any of his body the one time we had sex before.

Knock it off! I have got to get ahold of myself. Earlier this morning I was certain that I was getting fired, could my brain please get a grip and stop lusting after my boss? This roller-coaster is not what I signed up for when I took this job, thanks.

"You might pay the bills," I tell him, leaving the bathroom, "but I'm the one who keeps this place running, and don't forget it."

"You sound like Deborah," Jack calls after me.

I flip him off, knowing he's looking at me, and I can just barely hear him chuckle in response.

I go downstairs and start breakfast, which is coffee for both Jack and myself, then go back upstairs and wake Penny. She blinks at me sleepily, looking a little confused.

"Where's Daddy?" She sits up, patting the bed like he might still be here, just invisible.

"Daddy had to go take a shower and get clean," I tell her, smiling. "He fell asleep with you and forgot to get clean and into his pajamas!"

Penny giggles. "That doesn't sound very comfy."

"No, it doesn't, does it? So while he gets clean and into some new clothes, why don't we get ready for the day and have some breakfast."

Penny nods enthusiastically.

"Were you happy to see Daddy last night?" I ask her, helping her to make her bed and pick out her clothes.

She nods again. "Will he see me more?"

"Y'know what? I think so. I think he'll see you a lot more, now."

I don't like to make promises that I can't keep, or that someone else might not be able to keep, but I think that it's okay this time. Jack really did seem remorseful and I think that it's safe to tell Penny that she'll get to see more of her father, finally.

Once Penny's downstairs and eating with Deborah—who's now here to work on a project for Jack—and the coffee's ready, I head on up to check on Jack. It really can't have been comfortable to sleep in that awkward position in his clothes all night, on a bed that's way too small for him and nearly falling off the mattress, so I wouldn't be surprised if he fell asleep half-dressed on the bed.

"Knock, knock," I call as I enter the bedroom again. "Made you coffee and eggs—"

The rest of my sentence dies in my mouth as I see Jack standing in front of his closet wearing nothing but a towel. Damn, there's still a couple droplets of water sliding down his well-muscled back.

Jack turns to look at me, and I'm still gaping. I've got to pull myself together. I swallow hard. "Breakfast is ready," I repeat, but my voice cracks and gives me away.

Now I can see his chest. And oh my God, he really does have tattoos everywhere. They're on his chest, winding up to his shoulders, and a few draping over his back. There's nothing too far down his arms, or up his collarbones—nothing that a long-sleeved suit shirt can't cover.

This whole time, day in and day out, he's playing the corporate man while underneath he's the classic bad boy. I find my tongue sliding over my bottom lip involuntarily, an instinct as I gaze at him.

He's just really fucking hot, and I want to lick him all over. I want to trace those tattoos with my tongue. Maybe even bite and see if I can bruise the skin a little, making little purple marks appear over it as it blends in with the colorful ink.

Jack's grinning at me, and I just know he can see every thought I'm having written all over my face. "I should've known you'd like these."

He flexes a little, and I almost whimper, swallowing it all back just in time.

"You're all about the bad boys." He saunters over towards me, and I watch the play of water on his tattoos and bare skin; all of that muscle on display. "Should've known you'd go weak in the knees for a few tattoos."

I finally find my voice. "Those are not just a 'few' tattoos," I point out. "That's a hell of a lot more than a few. What did you do, volunteer to be a blank canvas for a bunch of tattoo artists at a convention?"

"I got them over time. Got my first one when I was seventeen and way too young, but I found a guy who didn't care about my ID." Jack shrugs. "Then I just kept getting them. I had to put them in places that a T-shirt could cover when I was younger, and then when I started the company I just kept at it, keeping it underneath what a suit wouldn't show."

"Lots of tech guys are supposed to be all cool and cutting edge," I point out. "You could probably get away with it."

"Maybe." He's very close now, too close. I could reach out and touch him, feel the tattoos for myself, and this is very dangerous territory. I should back away, but I don't.

"But I don't really want anyone in the corporate world to see these." Jack gestures at his tattoos. "These are the real me. Not the guy in the boardroom. Why should I let them see that?"

I nod dumbly. I should really leave the room, but for some reason, I can't seem to find an excuse or unstick my feet from the floor. "They're good. The tattoos, I mean. They're really beautiful work."

My hand starts to reach out and I clench my fingers, keeping it at my side instead. Jack stares down at me. "Would you like to touch?"

"I shouldn't." I'm whispering, and I don't know why.

"I really want you to," he admits, his voice just as soft as mine.

I reach out, running my fingertips along the curves of the tattoos. "I want to know what they all mean." There's a lot of them, some more typically metal like a skull with fire burning in the depths of its eye sockets, and others gentler, like a hummingbird done up in oil-slick colors.

"I could tell you." Jack's hand closes over mine.

I look up at him, freezing. His eyes are dark and hungry, just like they were that night at the bar, and I know what he's going to do, and that I should stop it and be the adult, but I can't. I don't want to.

Jack pulls me in with an arm around my waist, and I let him, and he presses his lips to mine, and I let him.

I let him kiss me.

Chapter 10

Jack

I was going to tease Haley when she walked in and started gaping at me. I just can't resist it. I like needling her, I like poking at her. She's fun to argue with, or at least, she's fun to banter with when we're not actually angry with each other. I like the sass she gives me.

But the look of hunger on her face when she sees my tattoos has me on fire. A lot of my hookups have seen my tattoos, obviously; although my colleagues haven't and I don't intend to let them. They're a bunch of boring spoiled snobs, why should I let them see the real me and these pieces of art that mean so much to me.

But usually the women I hook up with just react with something about how hot they are and then move on. Haley stares at them like they're pieces of art. Which, they are, but most people don't see them that way.

Her gaze skims over the shape of the tattoos like she's tracing every line of them. I can see her blushing, see the desire in her eyes, but she seems to find them not just sexy but entrancing.

I can't really tease her about that, at least not too much. I'm too busy being turned on by how much she likes them.

Yeah, Haley likes bad boys, and that includes tattoos, but she doesn't just like the shallow aesthetics. She likes what they mean, and the beauty of them. She seems to want to know why I got them.

My tattoos all have a lot of meaning for me. Even the ones I got back when I was a too-rebellious teen, mad at the world and only able to really express it through song. I try not to get them just because, but to wait until I have something that really speaks to me, something that has an image attached that I just have to put on my body.

The last one I got was a hummingbird. In some cultures, hummingbirds are viewed as the spirits of warriors, or as the souls of your loved ones coming back to visit you. I thought both were appropriate for Emily, so about a year after she passed, I got the tattoo.

I haven't felt the need to get another one since, but I'm sure it won't be my last. I enjoy the process of picking out and receiving a tattoo too much, I'm sure I'll keep getting them until the day I die. I just need to wait for the right idea to come to me.

But Haley's face... I can't help it. I'm drawn to the expression of awe and arousal there, and I want her. I want her so fucking badly. I've wanted her the whole time. And she's staring at my tattoos and enjoying them, and she just helped me see how stupid I was being with my daughter because she never backs down from me, not like everyone else in my life—

It's a terrible idea, but I can't resist. I kiss her anyway.

Haley gasps against my mouth, and I press her closer to me. Her hands slide all over my chest and shoulders, and I realize that even with our eyes closed and her mouth against mine, she's mapping out my tattoos with her hands.

It's fucking adorable.

I yank at her clothes, pressing her forward, but I can't kiss her and get her undressed at the same time. I pull back just enough to help her get out of her shirt and push down her jeans, and then I pull her back into me again.

Haley moans as I kiss her, her hands moving greedily down to rip away my towel. My cock is swelling with need, hot and heavy between my legs, and then Haley wraps her hand around it, stroking in long, sure movements.

I growl against her mouth and turn her so that we're moving away from my walk-in closet and taking the few steps into the bathroom. I have my gigantic bed, but that's too far away, and the bathroom counter is right here, right where I want her.

I get my hands around her thighs and lift her up onto the counter, spreading her legs. Haley whimpers and kisses all over my neck, down to my shoulders and chest. Her tongue swirls around my tattoos and I chuckle, turned on and amused in equal measure by how much she likes them.

"You really like those, huh?"

"So do you," Haley shoots back, her face bright pink. "You're the one who got them."

I laugh and then step in between her legs and drag her closer to the edge of the bathroom counter. Haley gasps as I grind against her, my cock moving through her slick folds but not getting inside of her, not just yet.

"Jack," she gasps, and then—"JJ...."

Fuck, hearing my nickname like that shoots through me like lightning. Haley laughs breathlessly. "Mmm, and you really like *that*."

She's got me there. "We all have our little kinks," I reply, and then, just so that she can't give another witty retort, I slide inside her.

Not all the way, just a little bit, but Haley gasps and then moans, her head falling forward and her teeth latching around my shoulder to try and muffle it.

I rock into her, my cock sliding into her more and more with each thrust. She's so fucking hot and tight, it feels so fucking good—just as good as the last time.

I can't believe I resisted fucking her again for so long. It was so good the first time and I wanted more of her then, I can't believe I didn't get her number. I can't believe I've held back this whole time.

Haley makes these delicious little whimpers as she grinds against me and I thrust into her, picking up speed. I want to take my time with her, but I'm so fucking turned on, lost in the feeling of getting to have her again. This is what I foolishly wanted last night when I realized she was waiting for me, even though I knew I shouldn't.

This is forbidden. It's not allowed. But that just makes it all that much hotter as I fuck her and draw all these delicious little moans out of her.

"You gonna come, baby?" I purr in her ear. "You gonna come from letting this bad boy fuck you? Those tattoos got you all wet and now you're going to come like a bottle rocket, so hard and fast, huh?"

Haley moans softly. "Yeah, yeah, I am...."

I remember how much she liked it when I praised her, the first time we fucked. "You want to be a good girl for me, don't you? Don't you want to be a good girl and come for me?"

Haley goes so tight around me that I almost come on the spot and I feel her hips jerk. Yeah, she really likes that. I doubt that stupid ex of hers ever praised her for any reason, especially not in bed.

More fool him. Haley deserves only the best. She deserves to be treated well, to be praised and spoiled.

"Be a good girl, c'mon, come for me, I know you want to, be good for me—oh *fuck* yes there it is, that's a good girl."

She's so fucking hot, slick, and *tight* as she comes around me, right on my cock, shuddering in my arms. I speed up, kissing her neck, telling her what a good girl she was because she is; she's a good girl who likes bad boys and it's so fucking sexy; I can't possibly hold back, chanting *fuck, fuck, fuck* as I spill hot inside of her.

Haley whimpers again and I jerk, feeling ecstasy wash over me. It feels so fucking good. *She* feels so fucking good. I swear sex isn't this good with anyone else.

We pant like that for a moment, coming down from our highs. Haley clenches and unclenches around my cock, drawing out my orgasm and giving me random shocks of pleasure.

I stroke her back. She fits perfectly into my arms, and it really is a shame I have to let her go.

But I do. That was wildly inappropriate. I'm her boss. She's my employee.

Fucking hell.

I pull back and clear my throat. "Sorry."

Haley bursts out into giggles. "Sorry—it's not—I mean it *is* funny—just—you gave me an orgasm and now you're apologizing."

"I'm your boss, we shouldn't have done that."

"I know, I know what you mean." She smiles at me, the corners of her eyes crinkling. "It's just funny."

"It is," I admit. I grab a washcloth for her to clean up. "I should've had more self-control. It won't happen again."

"Right." Haley cleans herself up. "That was—I was really into it, I mean, I really like tattoos in case you couldn't tell. But you're right, we shouldn't have done it. We can't do it again."

"Right." I clear my throat. "I'll be spending more time with Penny."

"Of course."

"We can control ourselves." Because spending more time with Penny means spending more time with Penny's nanny.

"We can," Haley says firmly. She rinses out the washcloth. "We're adults, and I'm not going to ruin your relationship with your daughter." Her tone and face soften. "I am really happy that you've decided to have a relationship with her, Jack. I really am. Thank you for listening to me."

"Thank you for being honest with me and calling me out."

Haley nods and we stand there for a second, a bit awkwardly, before she clears her throat and jerks her thumb over her shoulder. "I'm going to just...."

"Yeah, exactly." I nod and let her go.

I sink back against the counter and glare at myself in one of the mirrors. "You fucking idiot."

I can't let my lust for Haley get out of control like that again. I have to find a way to control myself, no matter how hard it will be.

And I have the feeling it really won't be easy to stop wanting her.

Chapter 11

Haley

I can't believe I did that. I'm fucking mortified.

Jack is my *boss*. No matter how much I like him, he's off-limits. And, yes, okay, he initiated it, but I should've had enough self-control to push him away.

I just couldn't resist. He's so hot, and he knows exactly what he's doing, how to talk to me and touch me. The way he slid his cock inside of me, like he owned me, and how it was so rough, he didn't even finger me first, it was like a backroom at a bar and yet we were in his fancy bathroom with the rain shower and the marble sink counter underneath my ass.

He's such an intriguing mix of buttoned-up wealth and control, and the rough, tattooed, rockin' bad boy that I crave; I don't know what to do with him. It makes my head spin.

I got to put my mouth all over those tattoos and lick and suck at them while he fucked me, and it got me just as hot as I thought it would when I imagined it moments before. He feels so hot and full inside of me, and he fucks me like he owns my body, not me, and he's going to make it do what he wants, which is orgasm. He's going to make me feel good because it's his and he knows exactly how to.

And the way he talks to me... I never thought much about dirty talk. It hasn't done much for me. I always felt a bit... bad, actually, because when my exes would talk to me, call me names or just stay quiet during sex, it wouldn't turn me on. Being degraded was part of the whole getting with a bad boy thing, right? So why didn't I like it?

Except—Jack tells me how *good* I am. He praises me and is pleased and happy with me during sex. He tells me to be a good girl and orgasm for him, and it gets me so damn turned on that I actually do, I actually orgasm from him ordering me to.

It's insanely hot, I don't even know what to do with myself. I feel owned and controlled by this powerful man who knows exactly what to do with my body, but I don't feel dirty or degraded. I feel precious, almost. I feel valued.

It's probably a very little thing to Jack. It probably doesn't actually matter to him at all. But it's the thing I've been missing in sex before now, with all of my exes. I might like bad boys, but I don't want to actually be talked to like they don't care about me. I want to be told how good I'm being, and praised.

Hell of a revelation to have about yourself when it's your boss.

I'm sunk. I'm absolutely screwed. How am I supposed to get Jack out of my head? But I have to. No matter how fast he made me come or how good it felt, I need to get him out of my head and focus just on being his daughter's nanny.

I really like Penny, is the thing. She's lovely. I honestly adore her. I like her more than any other kid I've nannied for, not that I would ever say that, where one of my previous clients could overhear me. She's fun and so very imaginative, and she loves dinosaurs and dragons, and reading. I'd do anything for her.

That means I need to keep my hands off her father.

I shiver as I head down the stairs to check on her. I might have cleaned myself up, but I swear I can still feel the phantom of Jack's cock inside of me. It just felt so fucking good, I can barely even stand it. I want to go upstairs and demand a longer fucking.

So far we've only had two quick rough fucks and it isn't nearly enough. I want him to fuck me for *hours*. I want to be begging him for an orgasm.

I take a deep breath when I reach the bottom of the stairs. "Hey, Penny, how's it going?" I ask, thinking only about her.

Jack's clearly not interested in a romantic relationship. He said that as much to me. Not only is he my boss, he doesn't want anything other than casual hookups. It's why he was so rude to me in the first place after we first fucked; he thought I was asking for his phone number.

It's all my fault for staring at his tattoos like that and losing my entire mind. I was practically drooling over him. Of course he's going to seize the opportunity. But while our sex is amazing, and he sure seems to agree, that's all he'd ever want from me.

And I want more from a man.

I want to be a mother and to have a lifelong partner who will help me raise our child. I want something serious and long-lasting. I might have had a hookup with Jack and be swearing off romance for a while, but that's just to make sure that when I do find someone, they're really a good person and not just the trash I've been dealing with before.

When the time comes, I'm going to settle down. That's what I ultimately want.

And Jack will never want that. He had his wife, and apparently whatever happened with her was so traumatizing for him, that it drove him to such a state of grief that he couldn't even be a proper father to his daughter until I yelled some sense into him.

How could I possibly compete?

I spend the next couple of weeks reminding myself of this, even while Jack takes time off work to be with Penny. He leaves for work late enough to see her off to kindergarten and comes home earlier than usual to spend time with her. He has to get work done in his office after she goes to bed to make up for it, but I can tell what a difference it makes for Penny.

She lights up seeing her father, every time. It's like this is a huge wonderful dream come true for her, and she can't quite believe it's real. I can't wait for her to get to the point where she realizes that this is real, and she can trust it. Her father is in her life now, and it's going to stay that way, at least if I have anything to say about it.

It's hard not to feel anything for Jack as I watch him play with her in the backyard, or drive her into the city to meet him for lunch on his break and see him crouch down to let her run into his arms, or watch him read her books before I tuck her in.

Now that he's accepted fatherhood, he's a natural. It's hard to imagine Jack not being good at something, between apparently being a fantastic bassist in a band (not that he'll tell me anything about those days); the leader of a billion-dollar company; and now a fantastic father.

But as if the universe heard my frustrations, I'm given

the perfect opportunity to remember that I don't belong with Jack and I never will.

There's an annual shareholder's party that Jack hosts, and since it's at his home, Penny will be there, which means I'll be there. My job is to keep an eye on her and distract her away from the party if it becomes too much for her. I'll probably have to get her to bed before the party's fully over too. Deborah warned me that the parties can go kind of late.

That all sounds fine to me. Free delicious food and I'm paid to watch Penny? No problem. I do let Sara get me dressed up, though. I want to make a good impression for the shareholders, and when she finishes with my cat eye makeup and helps me pick out a dress, I actually feel pretty damn sexy.

The dress is black, to keep it classy, and hugs my body. It's not leather, since that wouldn't be appropriate, but I still feel a little bit like a bad girl while I wear it for the way it hugs my curves, even though it's also elegant enough for a party full of rich people like this one.

We braid my hair, something that takes Sara a whole hour with how many curls I have, and we add the tiniest touch of glitter to my cheekbones. Just something slightly festive for the evening since it is a big celebratory party.

I twirl in front of the mirror, watching the skirt of the black dress flair. "You look so damn cute," Sara says, clapping her hands together. "I bet you're going to be the sexiest person there."

"It's not about being sexy." I frown at myself in the mirror. "Is it too much? This is a classy kind of party; it's all of my boss's shareholders."

"No, no, you look classy. You're just also beautiful. I doubt anyone else there will look so good."

There's a tiny part of me that is excited at the idea of

being the best-dressed person at the party. I know that I shouldn't want that. Jack is still off-limits, party or no party. But I do like the idea of showing myself off for him a little.

I want him to want me, even if I know he can't have me. It's a dangerous game, but I can't help myself. There's a little bit of a bad girl in me too.

I have to get to the party early so that I make sure Penny's ready to go; and when I arrive, I nearly run smack into a caterer. The whole place is in a whirl as hired servers set up the food, a massive ice sculpture, and other decorations to make sure everything's perfect. I'm pretty sure I've been to weddings that were less of a production than this is.

There are no less than three people on walkie-talkie headsets, giving orders and looking over things with a clipboard in one hand and a cell phone in the other, and I definitely feel a little intimidated.

I try to avoid everyone setting up and hurry up the stairs to find Penny. "Hey, bugaboo, are you excited for the party?" I call as I head down the hall to her bedroom.

Penny pops her head out of another room, the library room. It's literally a room that's full of books, some appropriate for her age, some for when she's older up on higher shelves that she can't quite reach. There's nothing wildly inappropriate in there, it's books like the "Nancy Drew" series or the "Chronicles of Narnia" stories that are more for when she's ten years old or so, rather than five.

There's a guilty smile on her face and I grin. "Was somebody reading instead of getting ready?"

"Daddy said I could read!"

"Mm, yeah, I think Daddy wanted to make sure you didn't get in the way of the workers." I grin down at her and put my hands on my hips. "You know how much we love your reading, but we do have to get you ready now."

Honestly, as much as she also loves playing outside, coloring, and all the other things that energetic five-year-old kids love, Penelope really would spend all day reading, if I let her. Sometimes I go to check on her while she's supposed to be going to the bathroom and find her literally sitting on the toilet, reading. Or I ask her to get dressed and she's on her bed, shirt off, pajama pants still on... and reading.

I'm pretty sure she'd forget to eat if I didn't have a rule of "no books at the table."

It can be a little frustrating sometimes, but honestly, it's mostly amusing and overwhelmingly adorable. I love how much she loves reading and learning, and I try to nurture it. I know how hard school can get, especially when you start out strong and then you hit your teenage years when you're overloaded with homework.

I herd Penny into her room so that we can put her in her lovely new dress. Jack wanted to get her something for the party. I keep reminding him not to spoil her too much, but I know it's because he feels guilty and is trying to make up for it.

Penny doesn't want anything other than for him to spend time with her, but running a company doesn't stop just because you have an epiphany about your fatherhood. Jack can't spend as much time with Penny as a typical working parent probably could, and it clearly eats at him.

I think a new dress for a party is acceptable, though, and Penny definitely loves it. It's dark blue, contrasting her red hair wonderfully, and she loves to twirl and watch the skirt swirl around her. She's so cute I could practically eat her up.

"You look beautiful!" I promise her. "Just like a princess!"

"No, like a fairy!"

"My mistake, just like a fairy." I get down on my knees so I can tame her curls a little and get them out of her face for the party.

"You look beautiful," Penny tells me softly, staring at me as I inspect her to make sure there are no sudden, hidden stains or something. Kids have a magical ability to get dirty every time you blink, even when they're just standing there.

Her voice is awed, and I can feel myself blushing. "You're sweet."

"You look like a princess."

"Thanks, sweetheart."

"Can I have sparkles too?"

I laugh as Penny pokes at my cheeks where the glitter makeup is. "When you're older, we can give you some sparkles. Sparkles are for big girls who won't get them all over the furniture."

I stand up and hold out my hand. "Shall we go?"

Penny nods and takes my hand, letting me lead her downstairs where the party is starting.

There are only a few people here, which is good. I don't want Penny to be too overwhelmed. I see Jack immediately, sporting a dark red suit that is just unfairly sexy on him—especially now that I know about all the tattoos that lurk underneath, where nobody but me knows about them.

I know he doesn't really think about it like this, but it makes me feel special, and sexy, being the only person who knows he has those tattoos hidden underneath his bespoke suits.

He smiles at his daughter immediately, and I hope I'm not imagining the way his gaze lingers briefly on me, as well. "Penny, don't you look stunning."

"She's a fairy," I inform him before he calls her a princess and makes the mistake that I did.

92

Jack grins at me, and warmth fills the pit of my stomach, rising up through my chest. He looks down at his daughter and nods seriously. "You're a lovely fairy."

Penny immediately twirls to show off how her dress skirt twirls with her, and Jack looks delighted with her very existence.

It's adorable, just how much he loves his daughter now that he's let himself. I still don't know the full story of his wife, but it's clear to me he must have loved her very much. He must have been so scared to love his daughter, but now that he's actually spending time with her, he just seems so much happier.

It makes my heart swell in my chest and I'm just so grateful I could be a part of helping it happen. And if sometimes I wish that I could be a proper part of it... it's just my wish to be a mother with a partner. That's all. I know I'll get it someday. Jack and I aren't—it's not like that.

He's a good man, he's sexy, and I see a lot of him because he's my boss. That's all.

Jack happily hugs his daughter and begins to show her off to the party guests who are already here, and I step away to the side. It's all older people, I notice, and just as I realize that, one of the older men—he looks to be in his fifties—says, "And who's this, Jack?"

Jack smiles over at me. "Oh, this is Haley. She's Penny's nanny; she's doing a fantastic job."

He sounds genuinely proud of me, and I can feel my face heating up.

"Oh." The man who'd asked about me eyes me up and down like I'm a boring piece of furniture. "I didn't realize she was the help."

My face flushes, but no longer out of pleasure. I want to demand to know who this guy thinks he is, but I force

93

myself to swallow the words. I can't make Jack look bad. This guy has to be a shareholder of some kind. What if I snap at him and that affects Jack's company because the guy's offended?

"She's family," Jack snaps. "And you'll talk to her with respect; she practically raises Penny for me because I'm busy at the office making you millions of dollars. Don't forget that."

The guy who spoke goes a bit pale with anger, and sniffs, turning away, but Jack smirks like he knows he just won the fight.

"I'm going to get Penny some food," I say and hurry away. I don't want to hang out around these people any longer than I can help it.

The thing is... of course I know that Jack is wealthy. How could I forget it? Every day I go to his massive house where his daughter has her own wing in the house, and so does Jack himself. He wears bespoke suits and drives a state-of-the-art car. I'm well aware he's rich. It's constantly staring me in the face.

But Jack doesn't act like most rich people do. He's kind and generous. He goes out of his way to help me. His idea of a night on the town is going out to some crappy bar so he can listen to punk rock bands play.

These people that keep coming into the party and adding to the commotion are definitely a lot more stereotypically rich, and they're all... well, they're all older than I am.

Jack's in his mid-forties, and honestly, I haven't thought about that much, at least not beyond the fleeting thought of how hot his confidence and knowledge is, and how I like the touches of gray in his hair, especially at the temples. He's going to be a silver fox in a few years, I just know it, and it makes my stomach flip.

But now, everyone here is his age, or older. I'm twenty-eight, which doesn't feel all that young. Honestly, I've started to worry about finding someone to settle down with so I can have a child before I'm too old and getting pregnant becomes a struggle. Right now, though? At this party surrounded by people in their fifties scoffing at me?

I feel like a child.

I focus on Penny and try not to really talk to anyone, to just be in the background. It's clearly what everyone wants from me. Occasionally guests will try to talk to me and ask if I'm so and so's daughter, or if I'm a new junior executive. One woman asks me derisively who's sugar baby or mistress I am, and I feel sick. Is that something that the other women are thinking? Is that what people are thinking of me at this party?

I'm not sure if it's better or worse when I explain that I'm Penny's nanny. They don't think I'm someone's mistress, thank fuck, but instead, the person will immediately stop talking to me, look me up and down, and say, "Oh."

Then they turn away and it's like I'm invisible.

Penny's excited to meet people and show off her new dress, and everyone's happy to meet her. Most people like kids, and it's impossible to resist Penny, although I have to wonder how many of these people cooing over her are only doing it because she's the daughter of the CEO who makes them all so much money.

I have to hover near Penny, making sure that she's okay and happy, but honestly, I'm more exhausted than she is by the time I'm able to hustle her off to bed.

Is this how Jack sees me? As some younger person who doesn't really matter?

All of the things that Jack's done and said swirl around

in my mind as I hustle Penny up and get her into the bath and ready for bed. Penny's tired, luckily, so she doesn't seem to notice that I'm a little withdrawn and quiet.

Jack told me that he's only interested in sex, no serious relationships, but he definitely has had sex with me more than once and seems interested in more, if only I wasn't his child's nanny. Would he make me his sugar baby or mistress if it wasn't for Penny? Would I just be some dismissed source of sex for him?

Does he see me as a child the way that everyone else does? Assuming I was someone's daughter or that it would be disgusting if I was romantically involved with one of the men there?

I feel so... worthless. So small. I feel like a moron, honestly. Of course, Jack would never think of me with the same respect and regard that I think about him. I feel like an idiot for ever thinking that maybe....

I know we can't be together. But I'd thought that he felt for me the way I felt for him—not just sexual attraction but a genuine appreciation. Affection, even. Now that we're not at each other's throats and spending more time together because of Penny, I can't help but be drawn to who he is as a person and find the banter fun instead of annoying.

I guess it was just stupid of me—no, silly, like a child—to think that maybe he felt anything more than sex for me. Now, surrounded by all of his shareholders and business associates, the people he actually spends all his time with, I see how ridiculous I was.

Penny's all ready for bed, so I get her tucked in. "Would you like me to read you some stories?"

Penny ruffles the blankets. "Can Daddy come up and say good night?"

"Of course, sweetheart. I'll go get him for you."

Once more unto the breach, I guess.

I head downstairs to get Jack. He's in the middle of some anecdote, and all the people around him are laughing. I can't tell if they genuinely find him funny, or if they're laughing because he's the guy who makes them money and owns the company and so they feel that they have to play up to him. It's all so fake it makes me feel sick.

Jack sees me and grins, and I hate how my stomach melts a little. "Haley!"

I walk over. "Penny's up in bed, ready to be tucked in. She was hoping you could do it?"

Jack's grin morphs into a warm, soft smile. "Of course. I'll go on up." He looks at the people around him. "Excuse me, folks, I need to go be a father for a moment."

He sounds so proud when he says it, like this is all new for him—and I suppose in a way, it is, even though Penny's five. Jack squeezes my wrist gently as he passes me. "Thank you, Haley," he murmurs, his voice low.

He moves away from me and up the stairs, and I fix a smile onto my face as everyone stares at me. "He'll be back soon."

"It's lovely how much time he dedicates to his daughter," one of the men—I think he's a board member—says.

I nod. "Yes."

"And you're the new nanny?" another man asks.

"Yes, I've been with them for a couple of months now."

"You seem young. Do you have a boyfriend? A husband? The last one did."

"No, not yet."

"Mmm."

Everyone turns away from me, as if they've decided by silent agreement that I'm not worth attention anymore. I wonder if any of them are judging me for not being married or in a serious relationship yet. That has to be it; that's why they're asking me, right?

I'm not dealing with this anymore. I head into the kitchen where the staff are. If I'm technically the help, then I'll hang out with the other hired people.

The staff is too busy to really pay me any attention, bringing out more food, refilling drinks, and cleaning up after themselves; so I just find a quiet corner, snag some food for myself along with a glass of wine, and eat quietly.

"Rich people, huh?" one of the managers with the clipboard and headset says to me. "The guy does this every year and goes all-out, it's insane. But hey, it means good money for us."

I nod. I want to tell her that Jack's not some rich asshole —that he might seem that way sometimes, but he's actually a good person, and when he is a bit aggravating, it's not because he's rich, it's because he's stubborn and convinced he always knows best.

But she won't listen to me, and maybe... maybe she's the one who's right and I'm the one who's wrong.

Maybe Jack's thought of me the way these people have all along.

Chapter 12

Jack

I fucking hate these shareholder parties.

I have to hold one every year to help them feel appreciated and celebrate our company's success. It's just one of those things that companies do and we're expected to follow suit and behave just like every other company. I smile and make nice small talk while everyone schmoozes to my face and I pretend that I'm not dying inside, and they pretend that they're not only being nice to me because I make them a lot of money.

The whole thing is a fucking farce, if you ask me. Nobody cares about me or likes me. They know that I don't care about them; I've never bothered to hide it. I don't like how these people care only about their private jets and how much money they can hoard, and I put up with them because I have to, not because I think they're actually valuable to me. I do my best to be polite to them, but I'm pretty damn sure that they're only being polite to me, an outsider who was in a rock band, because I made this whole billion-dollar gravy train for them.

So we exist in this strange place of mutual dislike hidden underneath politeness and societal niceties. Or they really do think I like them and that I'm *grateful* to be one of the elite, to be one of their equals. I'm not sure which idea I hate more.

Either way, here I am, hosting another one of these stupid parties.

At least Penny's having fun. Everyone's nice to her because she's my daughter, but she's too young to understand when the attention isn't genuine, and it looks like a lot of people just like her because she's adorable. I can't blame them.

I feel like a whole new door has opened in my heart. I knew that I would love Penelope, but I worried that all I would do when I looked at her was think about Emily. I was sure I would just see Emily in her, and feel pain and heartbreak all over again.

While I do see Emily in her sometimes... I actually also see so much of Penelope herself. She's a voracious reader, just like her mother, and she looks somewhat like her mother, but she also looks like me. She also loves fairies and dinosaurs, which are things Emily never much cared about. Emily was into computers and space, both from a young age. Penelope's much more interested in fantasy and fairy tales and history.

She's her own person. She's not just a combination of Emily and myself, but someone else entirely, her own little being who's exploring the world for the first time and growing every day, and so when I look at her, I don't see Emily. I don't see myself, either. I just see Penny, my daughter.

I feel terrible for having missed out on so much time, so

I try to make up for it as much as I can, spending as much time with Penny as my work schedule will allow. I'm head over heels for my daughter, as I think all parents really should be, and I just feel like a heel for having wasted so much time swallowed up in my grief and anger.

There's no way I'll ever be able to pay Haley back for the kindness she's done with getting my head on straight. Or, more like wrenching it on straight.

It's no hardship to watch everyone love Penny at the party, and it's definitely not a problem to disappear for a while and tuck her in. Honestly, I'm relieved she wants me to tuck her in. It's an excuse to get away from the party for a while, and it's a reminder that she really doesn't resent me or hold any of this against me. Penny just... loves me. That's it. She's five, and she loves me and forgives me.

It really is that simple to her.

Penny's waiting for me when I get upstairs, and she grins and burrows herself further into bed. I grin right back at her. "I heard there's a little dinosaur that needs to be tucked in bed."

"Uh-huh." Penny nods. "But, but, but the little dinosaur... needs to be read a story first."

"Oh, well, I wasn't told about that. We'll have to take care of that right away."

I pick out a couple of books and sit down next to her. Penny snuggles in close, and I begin to read.

Her eyes are falling closed when I finish the second book. I think the party really wore her out. But she'll get in reading however she can, no matter how tired she is.

I kiss her forehead and tuck her in. "Sweet dreams, little dinosaur."

When I get back downstairs, the party is still in full

101

swing. I'm not surprised, but damn I wish everyone would suddenly decide it's late and head home. Bedtime for Penny doesn't mean it's nearly bedtime for everyone else. It's only 8:00 p.m. after all.

I walk through the party, smiling and nodding at everyone but not actually engaging. Where's Haley? I can't see her, which is surprising. She's so full of life and confident that I figured she'd be the life of a party like this, charming all of these absolute grumps.

I shouldn't look for her. I should go and charm my guests some more, listen to their boring stories about their latest yachts. Haley's an adult, she can handle herself.

I find myself walking through the house, trying to find her anyway.

She's not in any of the rooms, which is odd. She wouldn't have gone home without letting me know, would she? Deborah's not here, because I know she'll be treated like crap as my personal assistant, but I grab one of the party coordinators.

"Hey, sorry to bother you. I'm looking for a young woman, she's wearing a black dress...." And looking sexy as sin in it. My eyes just about fell out of my head when I saw her.

Not that I can do anything about it. I've already lost control once and I can't do that again. I know how easily this could go sideways and I'm not going to let that happen. Especially not now that I'm healing my relationship with my daughter. I can't ruin things for her by taking away her nanny because Haley and I couldn't control ourselves.

But fuck she really did look amazing in that dress. It was classy with a fun little skirt, but tight at the top, showing off her breasts, and the hint of glitter on her cheekbones was playful—adorable, really.

"Oh, light brown skin? She's in the kitchen." The coordinator shrugs and heads over to another room to deal with some issue with the canapes.

What's Haley doing in the kitchen?

I head through the house to the kitchen and dodge the various catering workers cleaning up the dishes and serving the food. Sure enough, there's Haley in the back, sitting on a stool near the pantry and eating food on a plate balanced on her knees.

"Hey."

She looks up as I walk over. "Hey yourself."

She sounds quiet, and one thing Haley is not is quiet.

"What are you doing hiding in here?" I lean against the pantry door and stick my hands in my pockets so I don't do something stupid like stroke her cheek or twirl a lock of her hair around my finger. "I thought you'd be out there making all the guys try to see if you're available on Friday."

Haley gives a small, bitter laugh.

I frown. "What? What's wrong?"

"Nothing, sorry, it was just—nothing."

"Clearly it's not nothing. What's going on?" I frown. "You know that I don't think—I'm not saying I think you're some kind of social climber. I know you wouldn't sleep with someone for their money."

Haley sighs. "Yeah, no, they already think I must be someone's mistress to be here. Only reason why someone my age would be at this party, right? Since I'm not some rich person's daughter. I think I keep disappointing them when I tell them I'm the nanny; then they just ignore me because they don't get to make snide comments about me."

My eyebrows fly up. "They're ignoring you? I told them—"

Haley shakes her head. "You were sweet to say something earlier, but Jack, c'mon. I'm not a part of this world."

"Well, neither am I. Not really."

"But you have money and power so does it really matter if they like you or not? They like your money."

"It matters to me. You don't like me for my money. You've got no problem being rude to me when you disagree with me. It means that when you're nice to me I know you mean it."

Haley gives a small smile to her plate of food, but it doesn't meet her eyes. "Well, I'm glad that you appreciate that."

"You know I don't care that you're younger, or that you aren't rich." I cup her chin and tilt her face up so she looks at me again. "Tell me you know that."

Haley's gaze is on me, her lips slightly parted, has my heart racing. We're in the kitchen in front of everyone, and the reckless part of me doesn't care, but I need to step away. I need to keep people from gossiping about something that isn't even real, because it can't happen.

Especially since people seem to already be looking down on Haley. And that just won't fucking do.

"I care that you're smart and that you stand up to me, and that you're dedicated to my daughter," I tell her. "I care that you're responsible and funny and you don't take shit. That's what I care about. Not anything else. Understand?"

Haley's eyes look wet and when she smiles, this time it actually reaches her eyes. "Thank you."

I drop my hand away. I don't want to, but I have to unless I want tongues to wag. Everyone gossips, and it's the hired caterers in here, but they might say something that my colleagues can overhear, and the last thing Haley needs is people making further bad assumptions about her. "Of course. I like you for you, Haley, and I'm not surprised they can't see your value. They hate me, y'know."

"They love you. You make them a ton of money."

"Yeah, and I'm not old money, and I'm not one of them, and I'm not even a tech guy like Steve Jobs and all those others from Silicon Valley. I'm a good businessman who would rather be playing the guitar in a rock band. I'm not even a techie. I was just using my skills to help the real techie get off the ground."

Haley looks intrigued, and I remember that she doesn't know the whole story about my wife and me, but now is definitely not the time to tell her.

I hold out my arm for her to take. "C'mon. We're going back out to the party, and we're going to have a good time."

She takes my arm warily and stands up. "You sure it won't look awkward? A woman nearly half your age on your arm?"

"If anyone else thinks it's awkward, that's on them. I don't like you because you're young and impressionable. In fact, you're pretty damn far from impressionable." I pause. "Are you uncomfortable? I am technically old enough to be your father."

Haley laughs lightly and shakes her head. "Only technically, a teen parent. And no, I don't find it uncomfortable. I find the gray in your hair hot, honestly, and I think you've proven that some things get better with age. But I don't really think about the age difference." She falters a little.

"Until now," I finish for her.

She shrugs as I lead her out of the kitchen. "It's a little hard not to think about it when people assume the only reason you must be here is because you're some person's midlife crisis."

I snort and lead her into the fray of people. Several of

the guests immediately come up to me, but I see them falter when they catch sight of Haley at my side. I raise my eyebrows. "Something up?"

"Nothing, Jack, nothing at all," one of my board members says, his gaze cutting over to Haley. "I hadn't realized you would let the help stay after her job was done."

"Haley's practically family and I'm not going to stop her from having fun at a party." I give the guy my shark smile. "Besides, I thought you all would love to chat with her. Haley's the kind of woman I see you chatting with all the time."

Victor, and many of the other men in this room, have a bad habit of picking up mistresses or sugar babies, and talking to the secretaries like they think it's still the 1950s and they can convince these younger women to date them for job security. But I say it with such a genuine tone that it sounds like I really do think he's having intellectual conversations with them, and now he can't correct me without admitting he just wants to fuck them because he's a bad husband who's tired of his wife.

Victor opens his mouth, then closes it. "Well. Those women aren't... she's the nanny. Surely you don't spend all your time with the nanny."

"Of course I do, because I spend a lot of time with my daughter. Haley and I have become good friends, and I trust her to take care of the most important thing in my life. I'd say that means she's a woman worth talking to, unless you doubt my judgment."

Victor and the others trust me to make them millions of dollars, and were literally just praising me for doing so. He can't say he doubts my judgment. No fucking way.

Everyone looks uncomfortable now. Haley clears her throat. "Maybe I should go, Mr. Steele—"

"No, you're not going to leave because people were rude to you. This party should be open to you just as much as it's open to them. I expect all my staff to be treated with respect. They're the people who help me do my job. If Haley wasn't here to look after my daughter, I couldn't focus on my work and keep making this company a thriving success. I need to be able to trust her and like her so that I don't have to worry about Penny while I'm at work. I think the people who help me keep this company running deserve a party, don't you?"

I finally let the rage build in my voice. Victor and the other shareholders don't do any real work, but they reap the benefits. It's people like my personal assistant Deborah, and the rest of my support team like Haley, who keep this company profitable by giving me the assistance I need.

I may be the captain and the one steering the helm of the ship in the direction I want us to go, but I need my whole ship's crew—and the shareholders are just the passengers.

Haley stares at me, looking a bit awed. It's the second time she's looked at me like that, and the last time—with her fucking asshole of an ex-boyfriend—she kissed me.

I want her to kiss me. But I don't want her to do it in front of everyone and give people the wrong impression about our relationship.

I pull away from her slightly. "If you'd like to go, Haley, you certainly can. Let me get your coat and I'll walk you to your car. I appreciate you staying late to look after Penny today."

Haley nods, her shoulders relaxing in relief that she can get out of here. I understand. No matter how many rousing speeches in her defense I give, it doesn't mean she wants to stick around with these snobs.

I get her coat and walk her out the door. It can get pretty damn chilly in Seattle in the winter although the summer fires are becoming a bigger and bigger problem. "I'm sorry about that. I should've known they'd be dicks."

Haley shakes her head. "It's okay."

"No, it's not."

"No, it's not," she agrees, laughing quietly under her breath. "But I mean... I mean that's how most rich people are. I should've known it would be like this when I went into it."

"Have you had to deal with rich people like that before?"

"Not this rich, no. You've brought me into a whole new bracket." She winks at me as she puts on her coat and I open the door for her, leading her out.

"If I'm honest, though, it wasn't the money attitude that got to me." Haley sighs. "Everyone hired at the party was dealing with that and you really expect it. When it happens, you're just kinda like... ah yeah, that's how it is. You're ready for it even if it isn't pleasant."

We head towards her car. "So what did get to you? Because you're not the kind of woman that lets people get to her."

I know that's not entirely true. Haley's an intriguing mix of confidence and stubbornness and insecurity. If she was truly confident in herself, I don't think she would've let that shitty ex-boyfriend of hers run roughshod over her for so long, especially not *several* of them. But she's never had any problem standing up to me and giving me a piece of her mind.

Haley shrugs. "Just the fact that everyone's older than I am. They acted like the only reason a younger woman like me would be here is because I'm basically being paid to be here—through money or sex or both."

"You are being paid to be here."

Haley laughs. "That's not what I meant."

"No, I know."

She sighs. "It's just... why *would* anyone of their age be interested in someone like me anyway, y'know? So it makes sense. I just felt so young, so... unworldly compared to all these people, and the way they looked at me... like I must obviously be someone's plaything, like I was an object...."

She trails off and my gut tightens in anger—but also in worry. There are some older people that I invited tonight, but most of the shareholders and board members are my age, mid-forties. Perhaps early fifties.

Do I make her feel young and naïve? Do I make her feel like she's a child and not mature enough or smart enough to be my equal?

I'm not sure what to say, but I know that I've fucked up in the past—just recently with my own damn daughter. Haley's been a lesson to me in humility and growth, and if I'm fucking up in another way... I like to think she'd tell me, but what if she's less good at standing up for herself than she is for someone else, especially a kid? It would explain how she ended up in so many crappy relationships.

I clear my throat. "I hope... I don't make you feel objectified."

Haley looks at me like I'm crazy. "You just defended me, why would you think you make me feel the way they do?"

"We met when we hooked up. And we did it again."

Haley shakes her head. "We hooked up, Ja—JJ." She winks at me, using my nickname to set me at ease. "You want to have sex with people, and that's fine. People like that guy... they keep younger women on a string and once those women are too old, they throw them aside and get another one. They want a pet to please them and to spoil, and they treat women like toys. You never made me feel that way. You were honestly the best sex I'd ever had." Haley blushes, and I can't help the rush of pride I feel stirring in my gut. "But not—okay, yes, you were amazing but also I mean that you were the most considerate man I've ever slept with. I'd bet you my entire salary that those men aren't half as considerate as you are."

She takes my hands. "The people in there treated me like I was somehow less of a person than they were. But you never have. Even when we've been fighting."

"Even when we were fighting you were making me smile," I admit, remembering the way she'd break into my office, picking whatever lock I put up, so she could leave Penny's art and completed homework on my desk for me to see.

Haley's eyes go a bit wide. "Really?"

"Really."

"I thought you were hot as hell, even when we were fighting," she confesses in return.

It really sucks that she's off-limits, because fuck, what a pair we'd make. Not just sexually, but....

The thought nearly has me reeling back. I've never even considered the possibility of falling for another woman after I lost Emily. She's always been the only woman I've ever loved. The idea that I would betray that feeling and that connection we had and fall for someone else always made me feel sick.

But the idea of having feelings for Haley is odd in how *not* odd it feels.

We get to her car, and the urge to lean in and kiss her is strong. Haley looks up at me, her eyes big and soft in the shadowed lighting coming in from the windows of my house. The yellow from the lights contrasts with the soft silver of the moon and stars, and it takes my breath away how stunning she looks, like she walked out of a dream.

I don't even realize I'm leaning in until I'm startled by the feeling of Haley's warm breath ghosting over my mouth when she speaks. "Thank you, again, for defending me. You really didn't have to go out of your way like that."

"Yes, I did," I murmur. "And you don't have to thank me."

"Yes, I do," she shoots back, smiling softly, her eyes crinkling up at the corners.

"Any time you need defending," I find myself blurting out, "from a shitty ex, from one of my colleagues, from a random snob—you just let me know."

"My knight in leather armor?"

"If you like."

"I like it very much," Haley murmurs, and I'm torn between arousal and terror at the feelings swelling in my chest as I close the last few inches and kiss her.

She's just so beautiful in this dress and lighting; and in the darkness of the massive driveway with all of the cars, it makes it feel like we're sheltered and hidden even though we're technically outside. Nobody can see us or tell what we're doing if they look out from the windows. We could be the only people who exist.

There's also something scandalous and sexy about doing this, about the idea of anyone I know being able to look out and catch us at this, doing something forbidden.

Haley presses up eagerly into the kiss, then softens, then goes stiff again, like she can't seem to decide how she wants to react to it. I get that. My head feels like it's spinning too, and my body is flushed hot with all the things I want and know that I can't really have.

I take a small step forward, pressing her against the car, and Haley gasps. It's like she suddenly comes alive, clawing at me and hauling me against her completely, her legs spreading, her body arching.

She's desperate and so am I, because I want her all the fucking time and I can't have her—

I can't have her.

I pull away and start to take a step back. We've *got* to stop doing this, especially right now as I try to wrap my head around the strange way I'm feeling, the fact that I might actually be starting to feel—

I shut that down. No, I'm not feeling anything for her. This is just ridiculous. Haley's got a great personality and she's hot, and I'm just letting myself get carried away.

But even as I pull back, Haley gasps in desperation. "Jack, please—"

"You know we can't do this." I hold her at arm's length, even as she squirms.

"I know, I know, I just...." Haley looks almost frantic. "You get me so *wet* and I can't even stand it."

"*Fuck.*" I groan. She's just so gorgeous when she's needy, especially in this dress. I want to rip it off her.

"Please don't leave me like this." Haley sounds desperate. "You can't—you can't just start something and not finish it."

I kiss her again, sliding my hand up her leg, feeling her soft skin underneath my fingers. She's fucking gorgeous, and so eager and warm against me. It breaks my fucking heart how nobody's treated her well; of course she wants me... of course she wants the guy who actually gives her good orgasms and treats her well.

And I want to give that to her. I want to take care of her. I want her to feel so confident that no other man, whether it's one of my stupid colleagues or some random leather jacket-wearing poser at a bar, can make her doubt her worth again.

The emotion sweeps me away and I can't bring myself to pull back, kissing her harder and my fingers finding their way between her legs as she spreads them. "Oh, fuck, baby, you're so wet."

"Sorry, sorry, you just—you get me so turned on," she babbles.

"Don't fucking apologize," I order in a growl, and the way that Haley shivers from head to toe tells me she likes that the same way she likes the praise. Fuck, the way I could take her apart for hours and have her screaming my name if I let myself bring her to my bed....

But I mean what I say. I really do want to be the one to teach her to have confidence in herself. She should value herself. Men like Vincent and the other idiots at this party shouldn't even give her a second thought. Their judgments and snobbery should roll right off her back.

"Please," Haley whispers. "Please don't stop. Don't stop... if you stop I'll cry, I swear... oh fuck...."

I toy with her with my fingers, rubbing and grinding until I finally pull away.

Haley sobs with frustration, and I'm torn because on the one hand, we need to stop this, we have to stop crossing this line—but on the other hand, to leave her wanting right now just feels cruel.

I sink to my knees, and Haley moans.

I push up the fabric of her dress and drag down the lace

113

of her underwear, putting my tongue against her. Haley grabs on to my head, her fingers sliding through my hair, her hips twitching as she gasps and shudders. She's so fucking wet and hot for me, and it's intoxicating. I want to make her feel so good she forgets every bad encounter she's ever had, until all she knows is me and how good I make her feel.

Haley whimpers, struggling to keep herself quiet as I drive her higher and higher toward her peak. She grinds into my mouth, just barely swallowing her moans, and finally, her head is thrown back as I send her over the finish line.

Fuck, she's so goddamn hot.

I stand up and Haley grabs me, kissing me fiercely, her hand sliding down into my pants and pulling my cock out. She strokes me, her hand slick from how much I'm leaking, and I know I'm not going to last long with how fucking on edge I am just from eating her out.

And then she drops to her knees.

"My turn," she whispers, and then she gives me a wink and takes me into her mouth.

My mouth falls open and I swallow a groan as she bobs up and down. Now, I'm the one struggling to keep quiet as the delicious heat of her mouth and her wicked tongue work on me, and I have to bite down on my own fist to keep myself quiet as my hips jerk and I spill into her mouth.

Fucking hell.

Haley pulls off, spitting into the grass and wiping off her mouth. She looks up at me with a gleam of triumph in her eyes. I love that she's proud of herself, proud of how fast she made me come like that. She should look this triumphant more often.

I haul her to her feet and kiss her, glancing towards my

house. The party's still going on inside, and I don't see anyone at the windows, as if they could really see down into the dark anyway. We're safe, for now, but it's only a matter of time until someone realizes that I've been gone for a while.

"I should get home," Haley whispers.

"You should." I stroke her cheek with my thumb, enjoying the softness and warmth of her skin. I'm terrified of the way my heart does somersaults in my chest at the chance to hold her, but I can't stop myself, either, equally upset at the idea of being away from her.

I don't like this. I don't like this at all.

"Drive safe." I force myself to step back. "And, uh, sorry about that. It won't happen again."

Haley nods. "It won't," she agrees, but I can hear her voice faltering.

I can't really blame her. I'm faltering in my head as well. I have to be the firm one here. I'm the boss, I'm her employer, I have to have some kind of discipline.

Haley gets into her car on shaky legs and turns it on. I hurry into the house, tucking myself back into my pants and making sure I look presentable before I go in.

There are a couple looks sent my way as I enter, but I put a scowl on my face and glare right back. One of the wives, Eliza, approaches me. "Everything all right with your nanny? You were out there a while."

"Poor thing was near tears, and I can't blame her." The lie rolls easily off my tongue. I have no problem lying to protect Haley, especially if it means I can make my guests feel a little guiltier for how they treated her. "I had to give her a bit of a pep talk before I sent her home."

"Oh." Eliza looks chastened. "Well, I'm sure nobody really meant...."

She trails off, probably knowing that nothing she says is going to put me in a more generous mood.

"Excuse me." I keep my tone just barely within the realms of politeness and head out.

This party is winding down soon, and thank fuck for that. I want all of these people out of my house. I need to be alone so I can have my breakdown quietly and on my own.

Chapter 13

Haley

"How'd it go?" Sara asks as I enter.

"Um."

I haven't told her anything about what's been going on between Jack and me. I've complained about how Jack wouldn't have anything to do with his kid, but I didn't go into details, and I sure as hell didn't tell her that he was the hot guy I hooked up with at the dive bar a few months ago.

Jeez, that was months ago? It feels like only a couple of weeks ago I met Jack for the first time. And yet it also feels like we've been doing this dance together forever. It's a lot.

Sara's lounging on the couch in pajamas, clearly all ready for bed. She was probably waiting up for me because she's a good friend that way. She frowns at me as I stand there awkwardly, unable to fully lie, my thoughts too much in a whirl to even realize I would have to lie when I got home.

"Everything okay? Haley?" Sara keeps frowning at me.

I set down my purse and take off my coat. "I think I'm in a bit of a complicated situation."

117

"A complicated situation? You realize the last time you said that to me it was when you revealed that jerk cheated on you."

I sigh and join her on the couch. "It's nothing like that. It's that... everyone at the party was really crappy to me. Just absolute snobs."

"I'm not surprised. Isn't your boss a billionaire?"

"Yeah, but it was worse than that. The way they looked at me... it was like the fact that I'm only twenty-eight was a bad sign."

"Any particular reason? Did they just think you were in college still or something?"

"No, they thought I had to be someone's mistress."

Sara's eyebrows fly up. "Seriously!?"

"Yeah, but that wasn't as bad as it was when they realized I was the nanny. They actually treated me better when they thought I was someone's mistress. But either way, they talked to me like I was dumb." I grimace. "It made me feel really terrible."

"Yeah, I'll bet."

"My boss was really sweet about it, though."

"Your boss? The one you've been fighting with all this time? I keep waiting for you to give up and quit."

"He's... um. He's actually not that bad."

Sara frowns at me and sits up a little more. "Is that so?"

I shrug. "He's. Um. He's really great, actually. Now that he's listened to me about his daughter, I... I think he's a good guy. He's just stubborn and he's not used to people telling him when he's wrong. That's all. I think we misjudged each other."

Sara squints at me suspiciously, and, well, she's got a right to be suspicious. It was one thing when Jack was just a hot guy who was also a dick. I'm used to finding guys attractive who are assholes underneath.

It's a whole other ballgame when it turns out that Jack is a good guy. And it was one thing when he was a good father to his daughter, but now, he's also defending me and looking out for me, and I don't know what to do with it.

"I just hope it isn't a pattern," I admit. "Because if it is, then it's going to be so much harder to... he's really hot, okay?"

"How hot?"

I wince and Sara groans. "Did you kiss him!?"

"So you remember the guy I hooked up with at the biker bar...?" I explain everything briefly and Sara's eyes get wider and wider.

"Haley!" She lightly smacks me on the arm. "This is out of control! You're way too compromised. And not just because you two can't keep your hands off each other. You seriously like this guy."

"No, I don't. He's just hot and a good person." Even as I offer up my lame excuse, I can feel what a stupid lie it is. Of course I'm compromised. I like Jack. I genuinely like him as a person.

Honestly, I kind of wish that he did turn out to be nothing but an arrogant jerk. This man, who actually cares about me, stands up for me, and spends time with his daughter—making her a priority—is dangerous. Dangerous for my body, but I'm sure I could get that under control.

But this last time... I didn't beg him to kiss and touch me. And I didn't mind kissing him back because he's hot; watching him dress down a bunch of snobs is definitely sexy —he was kind to me and stood up for me; he didn't like how they were treating me.

119

Sara snorts. "Yeah, and you wouldn't quit because of his daughter even though he was being a jerk about it."

"Of course I wouldn't. Penny's a good kid and she deserves someone who loves her. I'm glad that her dad finally sees that, but if he didn't, I would want to make sure that there was someone who did, and I couldn't abandon her."

"But you can abandon a bad work situation, and you didn't have to provoke him. You went out of your way to do that."

"What's your point?"

"My point is that you're compromised. You care more about this kid than you should, because you let caring about her bring you head-to-head with the guy. I'm shocked he didn't fire you for your behavior and I think the fact that he didn't says a lot about what he feels for you."

I laugh. "Jack doesn't feel anything for me."

"You two have had sex!"

"And? He's all casual. That's why he was a jerk to me at the bar afterward; he thought I was asking for his number."

"So, what, he's going to keep telling you that it's the last time and nothing can happen, and then gives in again and sleeps with you, *again?* And it's never going to be anything more than casual sex? Are you sure he's not using you?"

I can see it from Sara's point of view. If our positions were reversed, I'd probably feel just as protective and confused about what's going on. She sees this guy telling me that we're not going to be anything serious and then he turns around and keeps having sex with me, then promising it won't happen again, and then going back on his word. He and I were butting heads before; and yeah, maybe I am a little too attached to Penny, but someone has to be. Up until I managed to shock Jack into realizing what a dick he was being, nobody was there for her. Her last nanny left her because of her husband's promotion, which is understandable; and the kid you nanny is not really your family, although the lines really can blur.

"Haley, you're a good and caring person." Sara takes my hand. "That's what everyone loves about you. It's what your exes always took advantage of. But it can be a weakness too, and I worry that you're caring more about these people than you should—more than they care about you, that's for sure."

"I just love Penny and she just lost a previous nanny she'd had for a long time. I don't want to leave her."

"And I think the fact that you feel that way is just another sign of how over-attached you're getting. Even if we ignore this whole... 'thing'... between you and Jack... how is getting so attached to Penny going to help you? She's not your daughter, and the moment she's a little older and can be independent, and Jack can just take care of the parenting himself, you'll be let go. You'll be gone, out of their lives. You're not permanent."

I know that I'm not permanent in the lives of the children I nanny. I've loved them all. But I've had to say goodbye, usually because they're old enough to go to school, or because one of their parents has been able to step up more and find the time to take care of them. A lot of the time I've been brought on when the parents have one young kid, but the mom is pregnant, and so they have me there until the second kid is a toddler.

But Sara's right. This feels different.

Sara watches me carefully. "I'm sorry. You look pretty shaken up, and I'm—I'm sorry I didn't mean to upset you like that."

I shake my head. "No, no, you're fine. I needed to hear

it. I think you're right. I just... don't know what to do about it."

"Well, you don't have to do anything about it right away. Definitely not tonight." Sara stands up and offers me her hand. "C'mon. Let's get you to bed. Things are always easier to deal with in the morning."

She's right. I nod and let her help me to my feet, taking deep breaths. Whatever this is, no matter how shaky it makes me feel, it'll all be easier to address in the morning.

It's just that I don't think morning will bring me real answers.

Chapter 14

Jack

Things are... not strained, that's not the right word....

Things are *odd* between Haley and me after the party.

She doesn't seem angry, but there's a distance, and I'm not sure what to do about it when in a weird way I'm grateful for it.

If it had been any other person—if it had been Penny's last nanny—I would have talked with her in the kitchen, then spoken to various people privately throughout the party, perhaps even sent a strongly worded email the next day. I wouldn't have gotten up on a soapbox like I did, in front of everyone, with the person in question right there next to me.

It was reckless and stupid and I'm honestly just lucky that it's the kind of thing I'm known for doing anyway so none of the people at the party got suspicious. I've never been one to behave like all the other members of the one percent, probably because unlike most of them I remember a time when I wasn't, and I have a reputation for being grumpy and stubborn.

Otherwise, people might've suspected there's more to it than just my usual dislike of the people I have to rub elbows with to get by.

I don't know what to do about how I feel about... Haley. And I think she can pick up on it. She's a smart woman; she must be able to tell that something's different. And she made it very clear before that she's not interested in relationships, especially with someone like me.

Oh, sure, I wear a suit and tie now. But that's not who I really am, and Haley knows it. She's seen the real me from the beginning when we ran into each other at that bar. She's done with "bad boys" no matter how reformed we try to be on the outside.

I just hope I haven't made her uncomfortable. I want to talk to her about it, but I think that would just make things more awkward in the end. I opt to try and keep a bit of distance myself and just follow her lead.

That's a bit hard to do when I'm trying to also spend time with Penny, but we make it work. I do have to be in the office a lot, or in my home office, so I do my best to spend time with Penny when Haley isn't on duty and has gone home, like getting her up for breakfast when I do and being the one to put her to bed.

Sometimes I can't manage it. As a tech company, we do a lot of business overseas, especially with the Far East such as Japan and China. The latter makes a lot of the parts we use for various technologies and Japan is one of our biggest buyers. The time difference means I have meetings at odd hours, and that's when Haley comes in handy to make sure Penny gets to bed or gets up and ready for kindergarten.

It's not the way it was for the few weeks before the

party; it's now more of an uneasy truce, but at least it isn't the arguing we had going on the first few weeks we knew each other. I'll take it, even if I'm not happy with it.

I'm in my home office getting some work done on a Saturday—it's unfortunate, but that's how it goes when you've got a company like this one where various clients and supplies are in wildly different time zones—when I notice there's a strange sound in the background, one that I can barely hear.

I get up and look around.

My office has a view of the backyard, but when I peer through, Penny's not there. I glance at the clock on the desk. Ah, it's her naptime. So what…?

There's that sound again. I peer through the window.

This time, I see Haley stand up, smiling in the direction of a squirrel in a tree. In her hands is a camera.

Oh, that's what the noise is. It's the snap of the camera. I hadn't heard one in so long—I'm used to people taking photos with their phones—I didn't automatically recognize it. It's quiet, but it's a quiet day, and I can just barely hear it when she snaps a photo.

I go outside, curious. Haley's focused and contemplative as she moves the camera this way and that, getting the angles she wants and adjusting the lens. Haley's usually so fiery and energetic, whether she's arguing with me or playing with Penny.

Right now, she doesn't notice me, and I can just stand on the porch and watch her as her brow furrows and she's lost in the serious art of capturing the perfect shot. It's adorable.

I completely forget about time passing as I watch her, fascinated by her fascination with getting her shots right. The squirrel moves on, but Haley seems focused on the trees that we have dotting the back area of the backyard, giving us privacy from our neighbors. Penny likes to play in them and pretend it's a massive forest.

Haley finally straightens up, looking down at the camera with a slight frown turning down the corners of her mouth, apparently looking through the various shots she got. I shake myself. I don't want her to think I'm some kind of creep or scare her, I just... couldn't take my eyes off her.

I walk down the porch steps. "Hey."

Haley jumps a little. "Hey yourself."

"I didn't know you did photography."

Haley looks down at her camera and smiles, then looks back up at me. "Yeah, it's a passion of mine. I had a friend in high school who had big dreams of being a journalist so she was on the school paper and they needed a photographer for the stuff that wasn't an official school event where they hired a professional. My dad had this camera he never used, I think he'd originally got it for bird watching, and so I volunteered and I found out I really liked it."

"Can I see?"

She holds the camera out and I step into her side so that I can see the photos without touching the camera, while she presses the button to slowly scroll through. I don't want to ruin anything by touching the wrong button on the camera.

"These are really good." She has a lot of fun with color.

Haley blushes, pulling the camera in close to her chest. "I have fun with it. Anyway, I just thought... since Penny's taking her nap, it might be nice to take some photos. Not for any particular reason, just... taking photos has always centered me. It's grounding, you know? Everything else falls away."

I nod. "That's how it would feel when I was playing bass in the band."

Haley smiles up at me. "Yeah?"

"Yeah. It was... my buddy liked performing, but I guess that's why you need a lead singer." I chuckle. "I was never in it for the fame, which is funny now because here I am, richer than I ever would've been as a musician, but for me it was all about the space where it was just me and the music."

"I love that." Haley pauses. "I'm sorry you had to give it all up."

"That's just how life is sometimes." I can feel her curiosity, her wonder about how and why I stopped and went into tech, but I don't know if I'm ready to tell her just yet. She's wormed her way into my heart so much already and I don't know that I could take much more.

"I was actually wondering," Haley continues, when it seems clear to her I'm not going to elaborate, "if I could ask for a weekend off? I want to go on a nature trip and do some photography. I thought it might be grounding for me."

A weekend trip in nature sounds like a wonderful idea. Actually, that could be something to take Penny on. A short little trip with Haley and me, see how I do with my daughter when we're not at home and I have to be even more focused on being a parent. "That's a great idea."

I arrange things for our trip, just something short to the Sequoias and Redwoods down further south, so that Penny can see the humongous trees. I think she'll be in awe of them. And Haley can get out in nature and have fun with her photography, and I'll take care of both of them.

When I tell them about the trip, Penny's excited, but Haley seems a bit odd. She smiles and nods along and is happy to be enthusiastic with Penny, but I can tell that something's strained. I can't help but wonder if I've done the wrong thing—but Haley would tell me if I did, wouldn't she? She's had no problem giving me a piece of her mind in the past.

We head on down on a Friday afternoon, staying in a chic little bed and breakfast, and sure enough, Penny's in love with the giant trees. She runs around and around them, shrieking about how they're bigger than anything else in the world.

"Can we bring one home?" she asks me as I carry her on my shoulders so she can see a little higher up.

"I don't think it would fit in our backyard," I point out.

Haley laughs. I can't see Penny's face, but Haley can, and she's grinning fondly from ear to ear. "Don't pout, Penny!"

I can picture so clearly the adorable pout on Penny's face, and I grin too.

That's when I realized what a mistake this was.

I took Haley on this trip because I wanted to because it sounded nice. But now I'm out here, watching her, with my daughter on my shoulders as Haley teases her and we walk along together....

Fuck, I did it again. I've made us a... a "family." This is the kind of outing that families do, the kind of thing I would do with Emily if she were alive and here to be Penny's parent and my wife—

"Everything okay?" Haley asks me.

I nearly stumble, which is embarrassing on its own, but when you're carrying a kid on your shoulders becomes dangerous. I keep myself righted and clear my throat. "Everything's great."

Haley doesn't want to be a family with me, and I shouldn't even want to be a family with her. How the hell would that be respecting my wife?

We finish our walk and I finally get service on my

phone back at the car park, so I text Deborah and tell her that I'd like to go ahead and deal with a current business proposal we're working on in person.

It's in London, Deborah texts me. *Are you sure?*

She knows I've been trying to spend more time with Penny, so I haven't been traveling as much as usual. *I'm sure.* It's only for a few days.

I'll get my head on straight away from Haley, then come back, and everything will be back to fucking *normal*.

Chapter 15

Haley

Whien I said I wanted to go out on a weekend trip, I'd meant *alone*.

I've been trying to avoid Jack as best I can. My photography hobby's been languishing and forgotten, I swear my camera's getting dusty, and it feels like as good of a time as any to work on the hobby as a way to distract myself from Jack.

Jack seems to be avoiding me too, or at least, as much as he can. With Penny, things are difficult. I'm grateful for her sake that Jack's spending more time with her; of course, I am, but I do have to say that it makes it a damn bit harder to keep away from him when my literal job is looking after his daughter and his daughter is the person he wants to be around.

He even spends time doing work on the computer in his home office rather than going to work downtown, which, again, is sweet, if it didn't mean that I have a harder time avoiding him!

I feel like I'm going to tear my hair out, and that's *before* he hijacks my idea to go to the woods alone. I asked him for time off. What did he think that meant? Instead, he brings himself and Penny along. And I adore Penny, I love her, and if it was just her that would be one thing, but it's not. It's also *him*. And he's the damn reason I wanted to go off into the woods in the first place!

When I'm doing my photography, I'm not thinking about the problems in my life. It all fades away completely and it's just me and the present moment, what I'm seeing through the camera lens. It helps me to feel calm and centered, the way I think people who do meditation tend to feel. It helps me find a sense of peace, and then when I go back into the "real world" I feel refreshed and better ready to deal with whatever's coming at me.

I did a lot of photography towards the end of my last relationship before I knew about the cheating. I just felt something was wrong, and I knew that I was unhappy. Now here I am, taking up photography once again, because of a man.

Great.

I can't stop thinking about the three of us as a unit. Especially on our trip. It's just a little weekend thing; I get my own motel room and everything—and honestly, I'm surprised that Jack, a billionaire, is okay with taking a motel room, like he's just an average Joe like the rest of us—but it's still not enough to stop the way my head groups the three of us together into a unit.

I don't know what to do about it.

When we start driving back, so that we can be home in time for dinner on Sunday, Jack clears his throat. "I wanted to let you know that I'm going on a business trip to London," he informs me. He glances towards the back seat. "I'll be gone for a few days."

"How long?"

"About a week, I think."

Definitely, the longest he's been gone since I started working for him. "Is this usual?"

"It used to be. Not... so much lately."

Jack glances towards the back seat again and I know he's thinking about Penny. "I'm sure she'll be fine," I reassure him in a low voice.

I want to reach across the gear shift and put my hand over his to reassure him, but instead I just curl my fingers into my hand until my nails dig into my palm.

Penny seems to have caught on that we're talking about her. "What is it?"

"Daddy's going on a short trip," I explain. "He'll be away for a few days, but he tells me that he's done that before and it's been okay?"

"Yeah. I guess." Penny doesn't sound very happy about it.

Jack frowns at her in the rearview mirror. "What's wrong, sweetheart?"

Penny kicks her feet. "You weren't a real daddy before. You were just like a pretend daddy. You weren't ever there. But now you're a real daddy and I'll miss you."

Jack looks stricken. He glances at me, a helpless look in his eyes. I bite my lip. I'm not sure what to do. On the one hand, it would be great for Jack to go, even if I'll also miss him—but the fact that I'll miss him is why it's good for him to go.

This is just infatuation. The fact is, I've just spent too much time around Jack. I'm sure that if I get some time away from him, then I'll feel better and realize that he's not really all that special, and I can stop mooning over him like an idiot.

I hate that I hate the idea, though. I hate that I'll miss him, and I hate that I hate that I'll stop caring.

My head's a mess, clearly.

"Well, of course I'll miss you," Jack says to Penny, still looking at me like he's a bit desperate. "But it won't be for long."

"Exactly," I chime in. "It'll only be for a few days, and you'll hardly notice! You'll be so busy with your own things! Like your friends and school and playtime...."

"But Daddy won't be there." Penny's voice is dangerously stubborn, taking on that high-pitched air that kids get when they're going to get really emotional and possibly even throw a tantrum.

Penny rarely throws tantrums, and in the car that definitely wouldn't be ideal. "No, he won't; that's true."

"Can't we go with him?" she asks. "Daddy can be at home and do work so why can't we play at his work with him?"

I wince. It makes sense to her, I totally get that. "I can see the logic," I admit.

Jack snorts in amusement.

"Your daddy's trip is really far away, sweetie," I point out.

"How far away? Like to the moon? I want to go to the moon!"

"It's not on the moon. It's in London, in England," Jack explains. "That's across the whole United States and across the Atlantic Ocean."

"That sounds so far away!" Penny exclaims, and for a moment I think she's come around, but then she says, "It'll be fun!"

I sigh and glance at Jack. I can already tell that he's going to give in. He's not used to saying no to her now that he's spending time with her. He's still in that guilt mode where he doesn't know how to be stern when he needs to be. And, well, I can be stern to an extent, but I'm not the parent, not really, I'm just the hired nanny. Jack is the real authority here.

I can see the conflict on his face. I don't say anything. How selfish would it be of me to insist that he go to London alone just so that, what, I can get over how hot I think he is and my inappropriate crush on him? That's on me, not on him. I'm sure he's picked up on my feelings, or at least I was sure, and that was why he was keeping his distance. But now he's taken us on this little weekend trip and I don't know that he understands at all.

That's a good thing, kind of, because it means that he doesn't realize how deep my feelings for him and his daughter are getting. But on the other hand, it means that he's not *helping*.

Jack sighs, and I know he's given in, even as Penny starts chanting *please, please, please,* over and over in the backseat.

"All right," he says out loud. "We can all go together."

"I'm sure you don't need me," I say quickly.

"No, I will. I'm sorry, but I'll be in meetings pretty much all day so if I take her, then I need someone to be with her during the day. You can take her to all the museums; I'm sure she'll love them."

I swallow hard. "Of course, Mr. Steele, whatever you say." I lower my voice while Penny cheers. "You will have to get used to putting your foot down. You can't take her on business trips when she's older and in proper school, not just kindergarten."

He sighs. "I know. And I will. But I don't see the harm just this once."

Well. That's his job as the parent. I'm just the nanny.

Deborah arranges everything, which doesn't surprise me, but I am surprised by how fast she does it. By the time we pull up to the house at the end of the drive, she's got everything sorted for our hotel and plane tickets. Sara's going to have quite a few opinions to share when she hears about this.

We leave the very next day, in the morning, and arrive in London at night. The flight was thirteen hours in total from LAX to Heathrow, plus the five hours it took us to get from Tacoma to LAX before that, so we're all absolutely beat by the time we touch down in England.

Penny's gone from excited to tired and exhausted to asleep and back to awake and energetic again. She's still tired and needs to actually sleep in a bed, but she's blearily looking around the airport excited to see what's going on. I keep a hold of her hand to lead her along while Jack gets our bags from the luggage carousel.

I feel like I'm dead on my feet, which just feels unfair, since I've really been sitting for most of this time. We were even in first class, which was nice; and I got a bit of a nap, but there's something different about being on a plane.

"You okay?" Jack's looking a bit tired around the eyes, but a lot more energized and focused than I am.

"I didn't sleep the best, and I've never been on such a long plane flight before." I've never been out of the country in my life, not even across the continent. "You seem fine."

"I've gotten used to it. Lots of business trips, lots of time zone changes... it's a lot, but if you do it enough you adjust."

"That sounds kind of lonely," I admit.

Jack nods. "It is."

I look away, unable to handle the way I can look into his eyes and feel like I'm staring right into the heart of him.

There's a car waiting to pick us up, and the driver takes

135

our bags and drives us to our hotel. I'm not used to everything being taken care of for me like this, but Jack treats it like it's just the usual, even though I also see him generously tip the driver. I'm glad he recognizes the people helping us and that he's not taking it for granted, but I don't know how someone gets used to there just being things here and done for them.

It is nice, though, just like being in first class was nice. A proper meal, plenty of legroom....

None of this is yours, I tell myself fiercely. This will be fun to enjoy for now, but it won't last, because I'm not a member of the family. I'm just the hired help. Jack will never want me as more than that.

We get to the lobby where Jack checks us in. "Hi, we have a reservation under Steele for the suite?"

There's going to be a two-bedroom suite for myself and Penny, and then a one-bedroom suite for Jack. It makes sense, especially since he has to be up early and go to meetings and we'll be pretty much on our own schedule.

"Yes, I have it here." The woman at the front desk types away. "The two-bedroom suite, for the parents and child." She smiles and hands over our room keys. "Here you are."

"For the parents and child?" Jack asks, picking up on something. His brow is furrowed suspiciously. "What's the suite, exactly?"

"Two one-bedrooms in the corner suite, with the pink child's bedroom? When I described the bedroom to your assistant she seemed excited."

Deborah must've misunderstood. There's been a mix-up. "It should actually be a two-bed suite and then a one-bed suite," I point out.

The woman looks confused. "I'm sorry, but no, that's not what we have reserved."

"Could we have another room, maybe?" I try not to sound too desperate. I don't want Jack to think that I hate him and I definitely don't want this woman asking weird questions.

"I'm afraid we're all booked up. We have a convention this week and two weddings."

"The convention is my fault," Jack mutters under his breath to me.

"Of course it is," I mutter right back.

Looks like we'll just have to make do.

"Are you sure there's nothing?" Jack presses. "I can pay—"

The woman smirks a little. "Are you a billionaire?"

"Uh. Yes, actually."

"Great. You can talk to the billionaire who booked this place out for his daughter's wedding, then, I'm sure he'd love to chat with you."

Ah. I look at Jack and wince. He winces too. "All right. We'll just. Take what we have, then."

Great. Just great. So much for not spending as much time with this man.

Chapter 16

Jack

I am tempted to find whoever booked this hotel for the wedding and ask him to do some room changeups, but I know how billionaires can get since I rub elbows with them all the time and they are not good at having their minds changed or doing things for others.

There's just a certain level of wealth you obtain where you're no longer connected to the real world, where you can't fathom that you have to sometimes be a nice person and that other people can have wants and needs that you need to accommodate or could conflict with yours.

I really don't want to have to deal with that.

But I do promise Haley as we head up to the rooms that I'll fix it. "I don't know how, yet, but I'll get it sorted out. I promise."

Haley sighs. "Honestly, it's fine, we're both adults. Neither of us is going to cram into the kid's bed, and if we tried to keep Penny from staying in that room I think she'd cry."

I have to agree.

"We're two adults; we can share a bed and not be weird about it," Haley continues.

"Of course."

I might agree with her out loud, but in reality, I'm not so sure I can control myself around her. I don't know how to have her in such close quarters and not want her; that's part of the damn problem. That's why I signed up for this trip in the first place.

But I couldn't say no to my daughter begging to come with me, and I can't take her without bringing someone else along. Deborah's got enough to manage, so I wasn't going to make her also babysit my daughter on this trip. The whole reason I hired Haley was to look after Penny, so I might as well take her.

Now we're in this damn mess.

"Besides," Haley continues, "it's really not worth getting into a pissing contest with this guy. If it's for his daughter's wedding, I don't see him backing down. Gotta have the best for his little princess and all that."

I get that. If it were Penny's wedding I'd stop at nothing to make sure that everything was perfect. I wouldn't want some guy coming along the weekend of the wedding and asking me to do a bunch of room rearranging.

"We can stick it out," I say out loud. Even though I'm not actually sure if I can.

We get up to our rooms and I use the key card to get us in. Penny gasps in delight as she enters the pink children's room, and I can't help but smile even with my annoyance at our predicament. Penny's bouncing on the bed, full of energy again, beaming wide.

Haley sets up our bags in the other room. It's night and we need to get some sleep if we're going to have a hope of not being jet-lagged. "I'm going to take a quick shower and then get Penny into bed."

"Good idea."

We get ready for bed mostly in silence, and I make a line of pillows along the middle of the bed in between Haley and myself. She eyes me. "Really?"

"You think that this isn't inviting disaster?" I point out.

Haley sighs and tilts her head as if conceding the point.

We sleep with the pillows between us, and my alarm gets me up early. I groan quietly to myself but haul my body out of bed and then head out for my meetings. I'm not used to sleeping with someone else in my bed, and I felt hyper-aware of Haley just on the other side of those pillows all night, even when I was in a fitful slumber.

I felt like I was sure if I took her into my arms I would sleep so much better, but I can't do that, and the knowledge feels like it's raking claws down the inside of my chest.

I get up, shower, get to work, and do my best to focus.

The meetings and conference all day aren't fun, but they're work and I'm good at it. I get periodic texts throughout the day from Haley, showing her and Penny going to museums and feeding ducks in St. James's Park. They seem to be having a lot of fun, and it makes me smile every time I get a new photo.

That's what keeps me going through the day with meeting after exhausting meeting until I'm free and I can meet them for dinner at Harrod's, the luxury department store. Penny's excited to tell me everything about her day, so I can just sit and listen and nod along while she babbles. It's adorable.

Haley smiles at Penny the entire time, clearly happy with her and the day they spent together, and just like when we went on our trip to the forest, it feels so much—too much —like a family moment.

I never felt that way with Penny's last nanny, but then again, I didn't let myself spend any time with Penny, so I barely spoke to her. She was also happily married.

Maybe that's the only difference. That has to be the only difference. This can't be anything more.

We get Penny up to bed after dinner and I feel ready to collapse, but I don't want my daughter to see how much this is taking out of me. Haley sees, though. Haley sees everything when it comes to me, and I can't seem to get her to not see me, to not see past my defenses.

"You okay?" she asks as I get my shirt off, relieved to be out of my suit after such a long day.

"I'm fine."

Haley snorts. "You're such a terrible liar. You've never been good at lying to me; I don't know why you keep trying."

Because I have to. Because I can't let you get close.

Haley makes sure the bedspread is comfortable, although housekeeping came by earlier. She pats the mattress. "Come here and lie down, on your stomach."

I frown. "Why? What are you doing?"

"I'm giving you a massage. I'm pretty good at them. Sara, that's my friend, she and I are roommates and we used to give them to each other in college when we were running ourselves ragged working restaurants, on our feet all day."

I shouldn't. I really shouldn't. But I'm still so damn weak where Haley is concerned. I crawl onto the bed on my stomach and let her gently straddle my waist so that she can get good leverage.

The feeling of her hands is amazing, digging into the knots, and I groan quietly.

141

"You really should go to a specialist," she mutters, digging the heels of her hands in. "You're just... piles of knots. No wonder you're cranky all the time when you're this stressed."

I snort in amusement. "It's not like I have a lot of free time. Running a company is a lot of work when you actually care about the company."

"I'm surprised that you care. It doesn't fit you." Haley sighs. "Sorry. It's none of my business. You just relax."

I want to tell her that it's okay to ask, and that I actually want to confide in her... but I'm so tired that I can't get the words out, and the next thing I know, I'm asleep.

I wake up with a jolt.

It's darker in the room. Haley turned off all the lights except the bedside lamp, and she's reading, some book that she seems to have picked up from the history museum she went to with Penny today. Her camera sits on the bedside table and I wonder if she spent time taking photos today.

"Sorry," I slur out. I struggle to get up to sitting. "I didn't mean to fall asleep on you."

Haley smiles and sits down on the bed next to me, one knee bent under her and the other leg dangling off the side. She looks freshly showered and is wearing one of the robes the hotel room provides. "You're fine, really. It was obvious you needed the rest."

"You could say that." I sink into the pillows.

"Is it always like this?" Haley frowns at me, her forehead adorably puckered with concern. "This... exhausting for you?"

"Business trips aren't fun. They're for business."

"Well, sure, I'm not naïve." She rolls her eyes at me. "I just don't understand. Most people who are in this life enjoy it to some degree, right? When I was at the party that was the impression I got. All of those board members, the shareholders, the other people who... I think they owned other companies? I wasn't sure."

She smiles, looking a bit embarrassed, as if it's a sign of stupidity that she somehow doesn't remember every single person at that party, especially with how horribly they all treated her. "My point is... you don't seem to enjoy any of this. The business. And I wonder why you keep doing this when it makes you so exhausted that you drop off in the middle of a massage like that."

"Massages are supposed to be relaxing."

"Don't lie to me." Haley's voice is soft, but I still recognize that look in her eyes. She's not going to back down. "You don't like the work. I couldn't see it when you were hiding away from your daughter, but now that you actually want to spend time with Penny, I can see how much you actually don't like work."

"Plenty of people don't actually like work. Why do you think so many CEOs just act like they're doing things while they really just zoom around the world in private jets and host parties on their super-yachts?"

Haley shakes her head. "You don't like this work. You could be one of those CEOs who doesn't care and just stays at home with his daughter all the time. You don't like those fancy parties, that crazy life—then why aren't you playing with your band and using your income to get gigs? Why are you putting yourself through this?"

I stare at her. I want to look away, but I feel like I can't. I'm a butterfly, pinned by her gaze.

And... I want to tell someone. I want to talk to someone. Not just anyone, but Haley. I trust her and I want to talk to someone I trust, and I'm finding I don't know anyone I trust as much as I trust her—because I trust her with my daughter. And it's kind of nice, that she wasn't there for everything with Emily the way my assistant Deborah and my bandmates were. I trust them, obviously, but it's nice that Haley has a clean slate. I can just... share it all with her.

"The company was my wife's, really," I tell her.

Haley's eyebrows shoot up. "Penny's mother?"

"Yeah. She was the techie, not me. I was in college to get out of my crappy small hometown and because I wanted to meet other people like me. It was just a way for me to have fun, to get out somewhere, and make connections for a band. I got a business degree because I figured someone in that band had to know what the hell we were doing when it came to managing our finances and shit."

Haley smiles. "Always so practical."

"I know it doesn't really fit the whole... bad-boy persona."

"I'm starting to feel like maybe I need to revise my criteria on what I want from a bad boy," she replies, still smiling. "I'm tired of the irresponsibility and the disrespect." She pauses, biting down on her lower lip. "So you... your wife was the one into tech?"

"She was a genius. And I wanted to help her. I fell head over heels and I knew that she needed help on the business aspect. A woman in this field? They get eaten alive. I wanted to make sure that nobody took advantage of her, so I made a whole plan, we graduated and got the company started."

"You loved her that much." Haley sounds sad, her smile faltering at the corners but her eyes warm.

"I really did." I sigh. "But it was a lot for her. I gave up my dream for her, and then we had this sudden success with the company... she couldn't handle all of it. She left me. Disappeared with a note saying she needed some time."

Haley's eyes go wide. "How much time did she end up needing? Is... is Penny—"

"Penny's mine. Biologically as well as legally. Emily showed back up... seven years ago, now." *Wow. Time flies.* "She apologized. She'd done a lot of traveling, working various odd electronics jobs, finding herself. She told me she regretted leaving me and panicking, and she wanted to start over."

"You forgave her."

"Of course I did."

Haley nods, her forehead puckered again.

"We reconciled, we were happy—we got pregnant and we were even happier. We hadn't been sure, at that point, with Emily's age. When it worked we were ecstatic."

Haley looks like she's in pain, her face screwed up. "What went wrong?"

"A pregnancy when you're older can be just as dangerous as a pregnancy when you're too young. Emily just... she wouldn't stop bleeding." I clear my throat, trying to avoid letting it crack. "They tried to do an emergency hysterectomy, thinking that if they could just remove that it would stop and they could tie it all off... but it didn't work and she bled out on the table."

My eyes blur and I wipe at them with the heel of my hand. "It was supposed to be the best day of my life and instead, I'm holding this carbon copy of my wife in my arms while the love of my life, the person who *should* be holding her, is dead."

Haley tentatively puts her hand over mine. "Jack. I'm so sorry."

I nod. "I couldn't look at Penny for the longest time. I kept my distance. She reminded me too much of Emily. But you were right that Emily would never have wanted me to put a distance between us like that. She was so excited to become a mother. She would have hated that I wasn't there for our daughter for so long."

"I'm sorry for the harsh things I said."

"No, you were right to say them. It jolted me out of the stupid headspace I was in. You challenge me like nobody else does. I'm grateful for it."

"So that's why you stay with this company? Because it's Emily's?"

"I have to make sure that her legacy is secure. I won't see this company mismanaged or go down the toilet because it was run by idiots who care only about their bottom line and how much money they can squeeze out of consumers. I want it to be a place where people get quality service and products and our employees are well taken care of. It's my responsibility."

"But it makes you miserable." Haley's voice is soft in a way; it usually isn't when she goes head-to-head with me about something. She squeezes my hand. "I like the guy who I saw out for a night on the town with his bandmates. That felt like the real you. The person I see the rest of the time... it's so clear that you're pretending. And maybe other people don't see it, but I do. I think you deserve to do what you want and be happy, not just spend all of your time driving your spirit into the ground."

I shake my head. "I was a terrible father who cared only about work, and I'm trying to fix that. But I can't just abandon my wife's dream."

"Maybe not," Haley murmurs. "But I think if your wife was the kind of woman you're telling me that she was, she wouldn't have wanted you to be miserable for the rest of your life."

"There are just so many things I could've done better. I

failed her in so many ways. I pushed too hard with the company in the first place and it made her flee. I didn't take care of our daughter for years. I can't fail her in this."

"Hey." Haley takes my other hand and swings her leg over so that she's somewhat straddling me, hovering above me. She squeezes my hands. "You are doing the best you can. You were grieving. You're not failing anyone. Penny's young. She's forgiven you, and soon all she'll remember is good times with you and what a wonderful father you are. Beating yourself up over not being perfect... that isn't going to help you. You need to give yourself a break."

My chest swells with warmth. For all that she's hard on me and calls me out, Haley also gives me such grace that I don't think I deserve, and I don't know what I did to deserve her. "You're a really good person, Haley."

She blushes. "Well. You're a really good person too, Jack."

Then she leans in—and she kisses me.

Chapter 17

Haley

I know that I need to keep a distance. I just couldn't help myself when Jack looked so dead after dinner.

The Jack that I know is always full of commanding energy. He's the person in charge of the space. I have no problem going up against him with every bit of sass and stubbornness I've got, because I know that he can take it and if his ego is a little bruised, well, maybe his ego deserves to be bruised after he's spent so long with everyone talking to him like the sun shines out his ass.

But the man who collapses under my touch when I massage him is so wrung out, I almost don't know what to do. But I do what I can to work out the knots and then I let him sleep while I take a shower and get ready for bed myself.

I double-check on Penny to make sure she's asleep and okay before returning to the room and climbing onto the bed. I'm not sure if I should wake him or not. I just sit there, watching him breathe, wishing that there was something I could do—and then he wakes up and I wish that even more.

I don't know how to stop the spiral of self-deprecation. I

think he's been in it for so long, disliking himself for so long, that he doesn't even realize. But his whole adult life has been making himself miserable, and for what?

Emily was probably amazing. Far more amazing than I'll ever be. But I don't know if she was worth... all of this.

Of course I can't tell him that. I don't know if he's ready to hear it; and I want to argue with him when he's less exhausted, and when I can actually go home to get away from him if it goes poorly, rather than being stuck in this hotel room with him.

He's your boss. His self-esteem issues aren't your problem. His grief over his wife isn't your problem.

I want to reassure him. My heart aches for him, it feels like it's hard to breathe; and I want to tell him that *I could be just as good for you as Emily was, I could help you feel better about yourself, stop working yourself to death, and let me be good for you—*

And I realize that I'm in love with him.

The thought carries me forward and I kiss him before I can think better of it; an instinctive movement, just wanting to give him some of the affection that feels like it's pouring out of my core.

It's soft. I think it's the softest kiss that I've ever given him or he's ever given me. Actually, I think it might be the softest kiss that I've ever experienced in my entire life.

I really don't mean for it to be anything more or for it to go further. I just—I can't help it. I want to comfort him and reassure him. I want to be *there* for him, I—I want to *be* with him.

I love him, and I just can't hold it in.

Jack kisses me back, slow and steady, and the kiss deepens. I sink down, letting him take my weight, ending up in his lap. His arms slide around me, holding me, and we just...

kiss, over and over again, the kind of slow and sensual making out that I haven't done in... ages. Maybe not since high school.

I had forgotten how *nice* this is. How wonderful it feels to be held, and to feel someone's hands on you, and to just kiss without any need to rush to the main event. I slide my fingers through his hair, feeling the strands silky against my skin, gasping as his tongue slides into my mouth over and over again.

Slowly, almost without even realizing I'm doing it, I start to roll my hips, and then build into a rhythm as Jack rocks up into me.

"What would I do without you?" Jack murmurs. It's so soft that it might be involuntary, and I find myself smiling against his mouth as I go in for another kiss.

His hands move down my back to my thighs, pushing up the plush, soft bathrobe until its bunched up around my waist and he can get his hands on my bare legs. My mouth falls open as I grind down and I feel the hard length of his cock properly for the first time since we started this.

Fuck, he feels so good. He's not even inside me and he feels so good. I don't know how I can give him up. Maybe this is just my weakness, forever doomed to fall for the guy that I shouldn't have.

Jack kisses down my throat, his teeth nipping at my skin, and I arch up, pressing closer into him. The fire in me isn't like the usual inferno it turns into when I'm around him. It's not a sudden wildfire. It's more like a fire in a hearth, slowly but steadily building as you add log after log to it.

We build up a rhythm, me grinding down onto his cock over and over, feeling the sparks fire up through my body and giving myself over more and more to the feeling of desire, *need*—and connection. Feeling connected to Jack, and wanting more of it.

I want to have sex with him, of course I do, but for the first time it doesn't feel like chasing a desire. It feels like... like sex is the only way to be closer to him than I already am. The ultimate way for us to join together.

Jack reaches up and undoes the tie of my robe, pushing it aside as we continue to kiss. His mouth moves down my body, to my breasts, and I arch up into the touch.

We shouldn't be doing this, but it doesn't feel like any of the other times did, where the fact that we shouldn't was a whole part of the thrill. Instead, it feels like we absolutely should be doing it. It feels *right*.

Like maybe we could do this every night. Like we're a family.

Jack helps me get my robe off and I toss it aside, his hands immediately back all over my skin. They're greedy but *slow,* and he takes his time, sliding them up and down, squeezing my breasts, sliding down my ass and in between, teasing my folds.

"It's not fair." I pull away and tug at his clothes, helping him get them off. "There we go."

Jack presses me down into the bed and I spread my legs automatically, cradling him between my thighs. He thrusts slowly, dragging his cock against me, and any other time I might chastise him for teasing me, but honestly it just feels *good* to feel his hard cock against my thigh, to relish the sensations. Not rushing to the main event, just enjoying the journey.

The head of his cock slips into me, just a little, like a teasing nudge, and I gasp and spread my legs wider. "*Yes.*"

Jack pulls back and then pushes into me properly, kissing me to cover up the loud moan that bursts out of me as I'm stretched and filled. *Fuck* it's so good, but we don't want Penny to overhear and wake up, ruining our fun and concerning her.

We lie there, joined completely, kissing slowly. I clench down, just enjoying the feel of Jack around me, how full he makes me feel.

Then he starts to move.

It's slow, rocking almost, like he can't bear to be parted from me even for the moment it takes to pull back to thrust, and I push my hips up into him in concert. We've had sex only a few times, but it's enough that now we have a good idea of how the other one likes to move, how the other one feels, and we keep moving together, pulling each other deeper and deeper under the flow of the water, until we're completely drowning.

Jack bites down hard on my shoulder as he fucks me in short, sharp thrusts, and my legs wrap around him, egging him onward. It feels so good, it feels so fucking good I can't even stand it, it always feels so... good.

We come at almost the same moment, gasping and arching, and it feels not just like the usual euphoria, but almost like—almost like peace.

I fall back onto the mattress, Jack on top of me, and the two of us breathe together.

After a moment, Jack pulls out of me, and kisses me softly. "I'll go get something to clean us up."

I lie there, listening to him puttering around, and then allowing him to clean me up. It's so sweet of him, and I can't help but wonder—after the camping trip and now this—maybe I've been wrong to fight it. Maybe I need to stop resisting it and give in.

Maybe we really do have something.

Chapter 18

Jack

The rest of the business trip is great. Well. Not completely. I still have to do my work, which isn't fun, but the rest of the time....

It feels like we're a family. Like it did when I took them on the trip to the sequoias. It was never like this when Penny had her old nanny; and sure, I can claim that's in part because of the sex, and also in part because I'm actually spending time with my daughter now, but I think it's more than that. I think it's Haley, I think it's the two of us.

I'm not sure what to do about it. I messed things up with Emily and caused her to run away, and then I never really got the chance to have much time with her. There's so much more we could've had together if she hadn't run away and if I hadn't pushed her and made her feel overwhelmed. Do I really deserve to try again?

Could Haley really be as good for me as Emily was, given the chance? Is it really fair to ask her to live up to the expectations that Emily set?

The guilt and questions swirl in my mind as we finish

up our trip and get on the plane home. Penny's exhausted from the trip, even though she loved it. I hope this means she'll be understanding when I don't let her go on the next business trip. I loved having her with me and hearing all about her day and the fun she had exploring the city, but Haley was right, I can't disrupt her life too much by dragging her all over the world. Especially once proper school starts. Her teachers aren't going to be happy if I'm yanking her out of class all the time.

I mention it to Haley once Penny falls asleep on the flight. "I apologize in advance for any temper tantrums you have to deal with."

"You could hire a tutor," Haley points out. "A lot of rich parents prefer to have their kids taught by tutors so that the kids can go wherever the parents need them to go instead of pulling them out of school all the time. Kid actors do it."

"Yeah, but I don't want her to feel isolated or disconnected. I want her to have as normal a life as possible. I don't want my wealth to make her spoiled."

Haley smiles warmly at me. "I love that you think that way."

"What way?"

"Well, look around us."

"We're on a plane."

"Uh-huh. First class."

"Yes, were you expecting me to settle for economy?"

"No, but most billionaires would take private jets, no matter how much damage it did to the environment. Instead, you chose to take a first class seat on a commercial flight. You don't buy out the restaurant, you just pay the hostess to get us a nicer table. You don't isolate yourself. And you don't want to isolate your daughter. I think that's admirable."

I clear my throat and look at the flight attendant walking down the aisle to attend to someone, my chest feeling a bit too tight for me to look at Haley directly. "Well, thank you." I desperately try to think of a change of subject. I'm still not used to being praised by someone who knows me—the real me—so well. "What about your photography? I saw you had the camera on the table while we were there— did you get some good shots?"

Haley smiles knowingly, but she graciously lets me change the subject. "I did, yeah, it was really fun. Penny was patient with me. I took a lot of great photos of her, actually."

"You know, if you ever wanted... I don't want to get in the way of your passions. If you ever needed to take fewer hours—now that I'm spending more time with Penny—so that you can focus on your photography, that's fine."

Haley looks a little confused. "No, that's okay. I can get done what I want to get done in the free time I have. I don't want to push myself too hard."

"Well, if it's your art, then aren't you going to want more out of what you can get just from snatching a few photos during Penny's naptime?"

"Not really?" Haley sounds even more confused now.

"You want to turn it into a business, right?"

Haley snorts, like I've just said something hilarious. "No. No, it's just my hobby."

"Don't be so hard on yourself. You're really good at it, you could definitely turn it into your full-time job."

"I'm not being hard on myself. I'm being honest. I just like my photography as a hobby."

I laugh a little, confused. "You don't have to lie to me. I'm not going to do one of those... artists are told all the time that it's not going to work out, and when are you going to get a real job, I'm not saying any of that."

"You're not hearing me," Haley replied, and oh boy, now she sounds angry. "I'm not lying to you. I just like photography as a hobby. Just because I'm good at something or I enjoy something, doesn't mean I want to make it my entire job. Sometimes making something your job, something you make money out of, is how you lose your love for it. It becomes a chore instead of something you do for the love of it. I don't want to lose that."

"You can't want to look after someone else's kids forever."

"No. I want to look after my kids, at some point. Being a mother has always been my dream. A stay at home mother, actually, but I know that probably isn't a possibility in today's economy, not unless I marry someone rich and, well, I don't know if you noticed but bad boys don't tend to be known for having a lot of money lying around." Haley folds her arms. "Are you going to tell me how to do that too?"

"I've messed up, haven't I?"

"You sure have," Haley agrees. "Just because *you* gave up your hobby for your job doesn't mean that all of us have that. Some of us like to keep both in our lives, like normal people. Some of us don't pretend to be someone that we're not."

She looks away from me, and we don't speak for the rest of the flight.

When we touch down, Haley heads home, needing a few days off. We already planned those days off in advance since I figured she'd need them after such an intense trip, but I have the distinct feeling that she would request them off if I hadn't given them to her already because she's pissed at me.

I can't seem to stop sticking my foot in my mouth around this woman.

Deborah notices that something's off at once. "Where's Haley?" she asks the next morning when I make her come to the house since I'm working from home.

"She's got a few days off."

"Hmm." Deborah looks around. "Where's your daughter? Kindergarten?"

"Yeah, I pick her up in a few hours."

"So what did you two fight about this time?"

I roll my eyes. "I gave her a couple days off after this trip since it was out of the blue and it's a lot to go traveling with such a young kid. Penny begged for it and I couldn't say no, but I did spring it on her kind of outta nowhere."

"And you think that I can't tell by now what you two are like? You were at it like cats and dogs for weeks, then suddenly everything's coming up roses and now you've got that same look in your eye you get after you would fight with her, while she's 'off' for a few days?" Deborah sighs and tilts her head at me. "Give me *some* credit, Jack."

I give her my sternest look. "Even if there was something going on, it's none of your business."

Deborah doesn't look chastened. I blame Haley for that. Deborah's never been scared of me. If she was she couldn't do her job properly. But she wouldn't challenge me. Then Haley came along and now she's got everyone following her example.

"Really?" Deborah's tone is mild. Unlike Haley—unlike most people, honestly—Deborah isn't one to get truly angry and raise her voice, at least not around me. She lets her words just speak for themselves. "So there's nothing that's gone on between the two of you."

I shake my head. "There's nothing that you need to concern yourself with."

"But I do, actually. I run your life, Jack. If there's something that's going on, then I need to know about it because I need to be prepared for the mess. It'll be my mess to clean up." Deborah pauses for a moment. "I'm not going to rat you out to anyone. I like working for you, sir, I always have. But I've especially liked working for you the last few months while you've been—since Haley was hired. I think she's good for you. So if something is going on, I want you to know that I approve of it."

"You shouldn't. If something were going on. Because she's my employee."

"You could always fire her and then marry her," Deborah says mildly.

I start in my chair. "Who said anything about marriage?"

Deborah doesn't continue that line of thought. Instead, she says, "So what's the matter between you two this time?"

I shouldn't tell her anything. I should keep it private. But maybe Deborah can give me some insight into what to do. "Haley's a photographer. I suggested that I could help her make it into a proper business and she got angry with me. I misunderstood her. And she said...." I pause. "She said that unlike me, she wasn't going to give up on a hobby that made her happy just because it couldn't make her the money she needed. She wasn't going to pretend to be someone she wasn't."

Deborah winces in sympathy. "She's very blunt. But if I can say so, sir, I think you've needed that for a while."

She takes out her phone and taps away at it. "You're very dedicated to your job running this company, sir. I've always admired it. But you know the saying: 'it's harder to start something up than to maintain it.' Once you have something actually running, it takes less work to keep an eye on it and keep it functioning."

"I assume this is going somewhere."

"I'm your personal assistant. I know your calendar. And I can tell you that honestly, you could stand to take some more time off. You don't need to be married to the office anymore. You're allowed to do things other than work all the time, and I think that—I *know* that you care about what your late wife would think of you. I think she would want you to be happy and not work yourself to death."

"So I think if you wanted to rejoin your bandmates and dedicate some time to that, even as a hobby... you could do that. I don't think you have to keep pretending to be just the businessman anymore. I think you can let the rest of the real Jack come out as well." Deborah shrugs. "Frankly I think it would be good for you."

I don't know what to say to that. "I'll... think about that. Thank you for your honesty, Deborah."

She nods and goes back to taking care of my emails.

I need to apologize to Haley, but first, I need to place a call.

Mark sounds surprised when he picks up. "Hey, everything okay?"

I wince inwardly. It's become such a thing that he always calls me to drag me out of the office, and I never call him, so the guy assumes it's an emergency if I'm giving him a phone call.

I need to be a better friend. Genuinely. Who have I become in the last few years?

"I was wondering if you would be interested in getting the band back together. Not professionally—I'm not giving up my company, and I don't think you guys want to give up your lives entirely either—but for fun. Casual gigs. That kind of thing."

I can hear Mark's grin through the phone. "JJ, my man, I genuinely thought you'd never ask."

Yeah, neither did I.

Chapter 19

Haley

I'm so fucking furious I feel sick over it.

Just because Jack has spent his entire adult life giving up everything of who he is to become someone he's not for, what, a woman who ran away from him? Abandoned him for years? Just because he's done that doesn't mean that all of us should too.

I'm allowed to just have a hobby. The fact that I don't want to turn my photography into a business doesn't mean I'm any less good at it or that it matters to me less.

I wonder if this is how Emily felt. Did she really want to get into the tech world and make a company off of her inventions and ideas? Or did Jack just assume and push her into it?

The man's such an arrogant jackass I wouldn't be fucking surprised if that turned out to be the case.

I'm so upset about it that I literally feel like throwing up. Actually, that might be a bit of a stomach bug from the traveling. I call Deborah and tell her I need some additional time off, and that I'm not feeling well.

She sounds a bit suspicious over the phone, and I

wonder if she suspects something and knows what's going on between Jack and me. She's smart and she's his personal assistant, she basically runs his life for him. If anyone would guess, it's her. I just hope that if she does know, she doesn't do anything about it. It's my problem to figure out with Jack, not anyone else's.

Sara's suspicious too. "Are you sure there's nothing you'd like me to know about?" she asks, following me around as I pack.

I'm heading down to my parents' house in Portland so that I can get out of the city. Mostly because I just feel that getting some real distance from Jack would do me good, and a little bit because I miss my parents and I think getting to be spoiled by them a little would help me out of my funk. But now I feel like it might be a good thing to get away from Sara's watchful eye too.

"No, nothing. I'm just... tired of feeling back and forth about Jack. He's just so damn used to... I don't know. The way his life is? I guess. I can't figure him out. I'm not going to keep having false hope that this is a fairy tale." I zip up my duffel bag. "I know that kind of thing doesn't happen in real life. He just—he opens up to me, but then he does something and I remember that he's spent his entire adult life being someone he's not and so how can I expect him to really... commit?"

"Do you want him to commit?"

"I don't know."

Sara helps me with my duffel bag. "Okay, answer me this: are you in love with him?" I swallow hard, and my emotions must show on my face because Sara sighs. "Yeah, you are."

"It's not like I tried to be."

"I know that." Sara lets go of the bag so she can hug me.

"Look, in my experience, if the guy isn't committing, then he's never going to. If Jack has some stuff he needs to sort out then that doesn't make him a bad person. He's older than we are. He's probably very set in his ways. But it does mean that you shouldn't have false hope, just like you said. So go see your parents, hug them for me, and get your head on straight."

"Thanks." I hug her back. "I know."

This is going to be fine. I just need a break, and to recover from this weird nauseous feeling, and then come back and do what needs to be done.

Mom and Dad are glad to see me. "It's been too long!" Mom fusses over me. "Honestly, that new boss of yours needs you way too much."

"He's really busy, Mom. He just needs someone to look after his daughter."

"Mmm, and when are you going to have a daughter of your own?" Mom knows that I want to be a parent and that it's a dream of mine. She's always been disappointed in the men I've dated, and honestly, I can't blame her.

"I just need to find a good man," I reply. "And I'm working on it, I promise. I'm just not feeling well and wanted to spend some time with you guys."

"Not feeling well? I knew that man was overworking you." Mom devolves into a sympathetic lecture as she heads to the kitchen to start making me soup.

It's good to be home.

My parents were always a little "helicopter," which I think is why I've been drawn to bad boys, but at least it's not too overbearing and it's because they care. Right now, I could use a little of that.

I just wish I could stop feeling nauseous.

The third morning I wake up and I can't even keep

breakfast down. I'm taking care of it discreetly in the bathroom when I get a knock on the door. "Be out in a minute!"

If Mom and Dad find out I'm seriously sick, they'll get even more fussy and I love them, but I don't need to be babied *quite* that hard.

"There's someone for you at the door!" Mom calls. "It's... Reed."

Oh *no*.

Mom and Dad do know Reed, since he and I were together a while and lived together. They never liked him, but that didn't have an effect on me. Long ago, I got used to the fact that my parents probably would never like whoever it is I'm dating, so it didn't register to me as something that was a red flag or a problem.

I heave myself up, rinse out my mouth, and leave the bathroom. "What does he want?"

"Probably to try and win you back," Mom mutters.

I head out of the house.

Sure enough, there's Reed, leaning back against his motorcycle. He smiles when he sees me. "Hey, Haley. I wondered if you'd—"

"What do you think you're doing here?" I snap. I put my hands on my hips.

There's no Jack here to defend me this time, but I remember how quickly Reed folded when Jack stood up to him for me. I need to just act like Jack did.

The thing is... Jack drives me crazy. But he still treats me better than Reed or any of my other boyfriends ever did. And the more I realize I deserve better from Jack... that means I deserve better than any of my previous boyfriends as well.

I deserve better.

I deserve better.

164

"I was hoping that we could talk," Reed explains. "I thought—well, that guy was a real piece of work, I don't know what he's been filling your head with, but—"

"He's been filling my head with the crazy idea that I might deserve better than a boyfriend who cheats on me all the time and makes me do all the chores," I snap. "I'm too damn sick to deal with you today, Reed, or any day for that matter. I can't believe you'd have the audacity to show up here—wait, actually I can believe it. Just...." I point down the road away from my parents' house. "Go away."

"Sweetie, you know that I didn't really mean it with any of those women! I love you, I always have!"

"If you loved me, then you would love me enough not to have cheated in the first place." I jab my finger in the air again down the street. "Now *go*. And don't come back. I'm never going to be with you again. I don't care if that means I have to get a damn restraining order against you to make it happen, I will do it. I deserve better than you and I always have."

Reed gapes at me. I don't know what it is about my tone of voice or my posture, but something must be different. He's always tried to run roughshod over me and this is the first time where instead he's just... speechless.

Maybe it's because I believe in myself, now.

If I can get someone as rich and powerful and smart and *everything* as Jack to want me, and want me over and over, then I definitely deserve better than what Reed can give me. Maybe I always have.

I straighten up. "Get the hell off of my parents' curb."

I turn and head back into the house without a word, strangely confident that he'll just ride away. Sure enough, I step back inside and close the door and I hear the engine of

165

the motorcycle gunning and then the purr of it as it takes off.

I sag back against the door, smiling in shock that it actually worked. Amazing what happens when I genuinely believe in myself and what I deserve.

Speaking of which...

I head into the kitchen. "Mom, I think I'm actually hungry for breakfast after all."

Reed isn't the only person I deserve better from. I'm going to go home after spending a lovely couple of days with my parents, and I'm going to tell Jack—I'm quitting.

Chapter 20

Jack

I can feel my jaw drop open in shock as I stare at Haley.

"You're quitting?"

Haley nods. "Yes. I'm sorry, I know this leaves you a bit in the lurch. But I think you also know that this is the best thing for both of us. You won't have a problem getting a replacement babysitter; Penny's lovely. Anyone would love to be her nanny."

"Penny loves *you*. More than she's loved any other nanny she's had. You can't walk away from her."

"I can, if it's what's best for her. I love your daughter, Jack, you know I do. Don't make this any more difficult than it already is for me." Haley's voice cracks a little and she clears her throat. "It isn't good for Penny for us to be going back and forth like this. She has to pick up on something, even if she's too young to really understand what it is.

"If we're going back and forth like this... she's going to pick up on it. She's going to notice. I think the only reason she didn't notice all the arguing we did before is because you never spent time with her. But we can't keep doing this. It'll hurt her too."

I run a hand through my hair. Haley's got a point. I don't want Penny to have to witness the two of us arguing or giving each other the cold shoulder. And we just can't seem to stop. "Look, I'm sorry. I was wrong to push you about the photography. And you were right, about how I—I haven't been myself all these years. I've been trying to be someone I'm not."

Haley's eyebrows fly up. She looks shocked. I don't think she expected me to ever do that, to agree with her on such a deep level. That... probably says a lot about me that isn't very good.

"You were right, and I've been miserable. So I contacted my bandmates. We're going to start playing again, just as a hobby. I can't do it as a career and I don't think my bandmates really want to do it as a career at this point either. I know they all have partners and families they want to start. But that doesn't mean I can't have what makes me happy."

Haley sighs. She looks less angry, but she still has a sad look in her eyes. "I'm really glad to hear it, Jack. Really. I want you to be happy. You've spent all this time...." She shakes her head. "I'm glad for you."

"I'm sorry I pushed you on the photography. I didn't understand. I thought it was... a matter of confidence. I know—your last boyfriend—you haven't been made to feel as good about yourself as you should. I thought that was the issue."

Haley does look bashful. "I... yeah I can see that. I actually—Reed tried to come by, while I was with my parents. I told him off and he actually listened." She smiles, shy but also proud. "It felt great."

"Damn right, it felt great. That guy's not good enough

for you." Even as I say it, I know I'm a hypocrite. I haven't exactly been good enough for her myself.

But what can I possibly offer her? All I've done since we started this was make her miserable.

"Thank you." Haley sounds sincere. "But I'm not going to change my mind. I'm still quitting."

"Penny needs you."

"She needs her *father*. I'm not her parent. I'm her nanny. *You* are her parent. Penny is going to be upset. That's not me bragging, that's a fact that I know about children, and they don't like it when someone they depend on goes away. She's had a lot of upheaval in her young life. I get it. But there's only one person who's going to be in her life forever and that's you, not me. Nannies go away; that's the whole point of them."

I rub my forehead and run my hand through my hair. The thing is she's *right*. I'm the person who's going to be in Penny's life. It's not like I'm going away. Haley is just the nanny.

It's just that Haley doesn't feel like a... like a "just" anything.

She feels like everything.

"I don't think I'm going to be able to change your mind, am I?"

Haley shakes her head. "I'm so glad that you're going back to playing in your band. I hope this means that you're going to be more of... yourself. Do more of what makes you happy. But we can't keep doing this."

"Is there anything I could do or say to fix this?"

Haley opens her mouth, then closes it and shakes her head. "No. You're a good person, Jack. Don't think that you're not." The corner of her mouth quirks up. "You're the first bad boy I've met who's actually not a jerk as well."

"Thanks, I'll keep working to bring the others in line."

She laughs. "I just... I want you and Penny to be happy. That's all. May I tell her? I think it'll be better coming from me than if I just disappear and make you tell her."

"No, that'll be the right thing." My throat gets tight. I want to cross the room and pull her into my arms, I want to kiss her and beg her to stay.

The last few days without her were miserable. Penny was sad and lonely, but I felt like I'd been run over by a truck. I hadn't realized just how much I wanted—needed— to have Haley around until she was gone.

But I promised myself I would never fall in love with anyone but Emily and that I would never go through that again. Emily was my everything; she was the reason I created this company. She was perfect.

Haley doesn't seem to realize I'm having a crisis. She smiles, nods, and then sticks out her hand. Like we really are just colleagues. "Thank you for everything."

I shake her hand, and somehow, I find a way to let go.

Then I call Mark.

"Hey, it's the middle of a work day. Everything all right?"

You know you're a workaholic when calling in the middle of the day gets you concern from your friend. "Yeah, I, uh, I have a problem."

"What kind of problem? Is this about the band?"

"No, no, it's about... it's about the nanny."

I tell him everything. How Haley was the girl I met in the bar, how we argued like cats and dogs, how we can't seem to keep our hands off each other....

"Wait, wait, wait," Mark interrupts me. "Are you telling me you might seriously finally be over Emily?"

He doesn't sound teasing. He sounds deadly serious. "I told you, I'll never be over her."

Mark sighs heavily. "For fuck's sake. I'm so sick and tired of this, man. I was hoping that when you were sleeping around that maybe there would be a woman among them who would compel you to—I don't fucking know. Actually, open your eyes and realize that Emily wasn't all that great!"

"Are you fucking serious right now? Are you telling me—"

"Look, I liked Emily. I did! But then she ran away. I thought that you would abandon this whole crazy company idea, but you clung to it. You gave up your entire dream career for her and she wasn't even there. And that was your choice and I tried to respect it, we all did. I know you making money from this company helped us out when we were having hard times. You've always supported us and been a good friend.

"And then she came back! And I was fucking pissed, but hey, you wanted her back, so I let you have her. I thought it would work out, she seemed really serious and apologetic; and you know better than anyone how Emily could be. She was so fucking vivacious. She was charming; yeah, she won me over! But then she died and you never got to actually put your relationship to the test and see if it would hold up."

I can feel my irritation growing and I start to pace. "Emily was—"

"Emily was a great person in a lot of ways. But you became convinced she was the love of your life and you never let go of that. You sleep with all these women and claim you don't want a relationship because the truth is that you're actually a huge fucking romantic, JJ. You're a romantic and you're convinced that you tragically lost the perfect woman. But Emily wasn't perfect! And if she lived —sure, maybe you two would've had an amazing marriage. Or maybe you two would've grown to realize you weren't meant to be, and you would've divorced.

"The point is that you don't know. And I think that instead of putting her up on this pedestal, you should realize that in front of you, you have a woman who from what you're telling me isn't perfect; but you aren't either, and she makes you a better person."

He's right about Haley making me a better person. That's true.

"You were Emily's faithful knight in shining armor. But with Haley, it sounds like she gets to see the not-great sides of you too, and she's still stuck around. I don't know, man, I could be wrong, but I know which one I think I'd rather have for my marriage."

I can't even quip back at him that he wouldn't know, because Mark is married. All three of my bandmates are in serious relationships that they've made work, so I'm actually the odd one out.

"She does make me better," I admit reluctantly.

Emily... Emily was a genius and I loved making this company for her so that her ideas could be celebrated and showcased. I wanted her to get the money and accolades that were due to her. But it was true that she hadn't ever... she hadn't seen me at my worst.

Haley has. By God, she has. And she's had zero problem telling me like it is for it.

"You said Haley's the reason that you've got a relationship with your daughter," Mark points out.

"If Emily were alive I would've had a relationship with her from the beginning."

"But Emily isn't alive, and you have got to accept that.

You have to let it go, JJ. Emily is gone. Does that mean you can't be happy ever again? That you don't deserve to be happy? You gave up the band because, what, you thought that you had to do it as this big grand romantic gesture; and then you beat yourself up for Emily running away, so you never went back? Has it occurred to you that maybe Emily ran away not because of anything you did but because she had her own damn problems?"

I don't know what to say to that. I'm speechless. Just listening to what Mark is telling me. My oldest friend, and someone who, I'm realizing, has held his tongue for years because I wouldn't listen.

It took Haley to get me to listen to the people around me. To stop doing any bullheaded thing I wanted and stop being such a goddamn arrogant jerk.

Mark sighs. "Look. I know that there's a risk when you fall in love. There's a chance that the person isn't going to love you back or that the relationship will fall apart. But that's the risk you take when it comes to love. I think you're worth the risk and I think Haley is too, from everything that you've told me."

"You think I should go for it?"

"Why shouldn't you?"

"I don't know. She's almost twenty years younger than I am, she was my employee, and I've pretty much jerked her around the entire time?"

"She's old enough to be an independent adult and make her own damn choices, JJ, and it sounds to me like what she wants to choose is you. And yeah, you were kind of jerking her around, but it's not like she was any less... lost. I think you both need to just talk about how you fucking feel. Y'know, like adults?"

"Ha, ha, ha."

"I'm serious. You deserve a chance at happiness, because you really have not been happy the last few years. Let yourself take it. Let go of Emily. Be with Haley."

He hangs up on me, which is probably fair of him. I stare down at the phone.

Let yourself be happy.

Dare I?

Chapter 21

Haley

Penny's up in her room, reading as usual on the bed. I smile as I enter. "Hey, sweetheart."

"Haley!" Penny springs up off the bed and rushes over to me, hugging me. "I missed you!"

"I missed you, so much." I drop to my knees and hug her tightly. This will be possibly the last time I ever see her, and tears spring into my eyes.

I try hard to swallow them down. I don't want to make this any harder for Penny than I know it already will be. But it's like they're uncontrollable.

"Listen." I pull back and smile at her through the tears.

Penny gasps. "You're crying!"

"I am, sweet girl. I'm crying because I'm sad." I take a deep breath. "I'm going to have to say goodbye."

Penny frowns at me. "Why?"

"Because I'm not going to be your nanny anymore?"

"Why?"

"Because I can't be."

"Why?"

"Because sometimes people have to say goodbye and

175

there's no reason why; it's just how it is. And it's sad and it hurts, but you're going to be okay."

Penny looks like she might start crying too, which makes me feel even worse. "When my mama went away, Daddy wasn't happy. And then you came here, and now if you leave, he might not be my daddy anymore."

"No, no! The reason that I'm able to leave is because I know that he'll still be a good daddy to you. He loves you, I promise you that."

Penny doesn't look completely convinced, and I don't blame her. But what else can I do? There's nothing I can say to reassure her. Jack will just have to keep proving to her that he's here for good.

I wipe my eyes. I know that Penny's not mine, but I love her so much; it feels like I'm saying goodbye to my own child.

That's part of why this is a good thing, that I'm leaving. I can't cross that line or let it blur. I know that it's hard for all nannies, especially when the parents are distant. You can't help but in some way think of the kid as yours and then....

But I've always kept that line firm and clear in my head with all the other kids I've nannied for. It's just—Penny's special.

"I love you, so much," I promise her. "I always will...."

My tears well up again and I can barely contain my sob. "So I'm going to have to ask you to be a good girl for your dad, okay? He loves you so much. I promise you. He's gonna be around now. You might get a new nanny for when he has to work, so I hope you'll be good for whoever he or she is, okay?"

Personally I kind of hope, selfishly, that Jack hires a male nanny. Not that it's any of my business and I know he never slept with any of the previous nannies, but still, I can't help the jealousy that spikes in my chest at the idea of another woman taking my place, both in Penny's life and in Jack's.

This is exactly why I need to quit. I'm not thinking objectively anymore. I'm thinking of them as my real family when they're not.

Penny nods. "I'll be good. I promise."

"Good girl. I know you will be." I hug her tightly one more time. "I love you so much."

Once I'm in my car, I burst into uncontrollable tears. I drive home in a blur, sobbing the entire time.

It's actually... kind of concerning that I can't stop crying.

I can be emotional, but I'm not usually this out of control. I feel awful leaving Penny; it hurts my heart like nothing else, honestly worse than my breakup with Reed. But I don't remember crying this hard for this long when I found Reed cheating. Maybe my period's coming on and that's—

Wait.

I nearly slam on the brakes out of instinct and force myself to take deep breaths. My period. It's late, by two weeks? More? I don't remember.

I find the nearest pharmacy, pull in, and check my calendar. Oh fuck, I'm really late. And then when I was with my parents, I felt weirdly nauseous... but I hadn't had a fever or a cough. I hadn't thought much about it. I'd been distracted by my frustration over Jack and then my damn ex-boyfriend showing up. But now....

I buy a pregnancy test and hurry the rest of the way home. Sara's not back from work yet, which is a relief. I lock myself in the bathroom and take the test.

My knee is bouncing with anxiety as I sit on the edge of

the tub and wait for the results. Maybe I'm wrong. Maybe I marked my last period down late. Maybe the nausea was something else, some kind of food poisoning. Maybe....

I pick up the pregnancy test and look at it.

Two lines. I'm pregnant.

Oh no.

I sit there, feeling almost numb with shock. I haven't had sex with anyone besides Jack since I broke up with Reed, and the two of us hadn't had sex in a while before our breakup; thank goodness or I might've been in danger of getting something because of all his cheating. That means—it has to be Jack's baby.

There's the sound of the front door opening and closing. "I saw your car," Sara calls out. "What are you doing home so early? Haley?"

"I'm in here," I manage to croak. I stagger to my feet and unlock the door, opening it up and holding out the pregnancy test.

Sara stares down at it, then looks up at me. "Oh."

"Yeah." I sink back down to sit on the edge of the tub and put my head in my hands. "I'm the world's stupidest person."

"No, no, you're not!" Sara sits down next to me and puts her arm around my shoulders. "You're okay. This kind of thing happens to everyone all the time."

"What do I do? I have to tell him, don't I?" I look up at her.

Sara makes a face. "Well...."

"What? He's a great father."

"It's not that. It's just—you remember how everyone treated you at that party he hosted. What'll happen when they find out you're pregnant? They'll claim you baby trapped him."

The very idea makes me sick. The people at that party treated me like trash, they *would* accuse me of doing something like that in order to get a rich payout.

I must turn a little green because Sara's eyebrows fly up. "Okay, let me get you some water."

She guides me to the couch and helps me get some ice water. I sip it slowly. "I don't like the idea of lying to him."

"Would he want to be a father again?"

"I don't know." He only just accepted being a father to Penelope; maybe being a father again, especially since he's in his forties, would upset him. Maybe he would feel it was too much.

He's finally going back to playing with his band, finding his joy, and his hobbies again. How would a new child ruin that? Because it would ruin that, wouldn't it? He would have to give up the band again so that he could be there for me and I could never, ever make him resent me like that.

I start to cry. "Oh, honey." Sara holds me tightly.

"I want to be a mother. I just... I didn't want it like this." I wanted to be married, I wanted a partner to help me raise my child.

Sara rubs my back. "I know, honey. I'll do whatever it takes to help you, you know that."

"I appreciate it, really." I pull back. "But I think the best thing to do will be to move in with my parents once the baby is born. Obviously, I have some time, I won't have to move in with them right away, so we'll find you a new roommate. And Jack was paying me well enough so I can help you with rent and stuff without working for a bit."

The fact that I don't have to go and get a new job immediately is a load off my mind. I can't live off my savings forever, but Jack paid me generously; I can definitely leave Sara with enough money to live on her own for a few months and not rush to find a roommate who might be crappy, or even find a new place for just one person if she'd like to live alone.

"My parents would love to help with the baby." They'll give me the emotional support I need, and the financial support. Raising a kid is a lot and I want to be able to actually spend the first couple years with my child instead of working 24/7.

Sara nods. "I know they will. Whatever you think is best."

I take her hands. "I'm sorry. I know that none of this is what you or I planned."

"Life just happens." Sara searches my face. "Are you sure you don't want to tell him?"

I think about it. Of course, part of me really would like to tell him. Now that Jack has given himself the grace to be a father, he's a fantastic one. I would love to give him the chance to be there for all the little early moments he missed with Penny because he couldn't bear to see her. I think Penny would love a little sibling too.

But I know what everyone would say about me. And I won't let Jack give up the life he's just now reclaiming. His life with Emily proved that he's far too self-sacrificing for his own good. I'm not going to let that happen with me.

"I'm sure," I say out loud.

Jack can never know.

Chapter 22

Jack

Haley's not leaving immediately, of course.

She has a week of watching Penny while Deborah interviews new nannies. I've actually asked Deborah to look into some men instead. I don't think that I'll fall for another nanny. I've never mixed business and pleasure like that before and Haley is truly one of a kind. But I... I don't want Penny to feel I'm *replacing* Haley.

Having her new nanny be a man will help with that. The idea of another woman taking Haley's place just... it feels too wrong to me.

But in the meantime, Haley's finishing up her time here and I've been keeping my distance, trying to sort out my own emotions. Thinking about what Mark said.

When I think about Emily, do I think of an ideal? The perfect woman who doesn't really necessarily exist?

When I look at my life, compared to how long Emily was actually in it... she really wasn't there for that long. She's been out of it, both from her running away and her death, far more than she's been in it. Could it be that really all this time I was devoted to an idea more than an actual person?

With Emily, I gave up who I was in order to be with her and give her what I felt she wanted. With Haley... Haley likes who I really am. She loves my tattoos. One of the first things she did was try to ask me if she could listen to my band's music. She likes the part of me that the rest of the world doesn't want and rolls their eyes at, the part that I've had to ignore for all of these years.

Call it cliché, but she makes me feel young again. She's found that person that I thought I had to walk away from when I was even younger than she is.

Maybe... maybe I do deserve to give this a shot. Maybe Mark is right, and I should let this go.

Maybe I should let myself be in love.

But if I'm going to do this, I'm going to do it right. I'm not going to half-ass it. Haley deserves only the best after all the jerking around I've put her through. I'm going to give her a romantic evening—our kind of romantic.

I wait until she finishes watching Penny for the day, and she comes down to the foyer. "How's she taking it?" I ask.

Haley sighs and grabs her purse. "She's still upset. I don't know how to help her. Was she like this when the last nanny had to quit?"

"No, she was a lot calmer."

"I think I've managed to convince her that you won't go back to ignoring her once I leave."

That makes me feel like someone's stabbed me right in the solar plexus. "I won't."

"I know." Haley smiles at me sadly and puts on her shoes. "But she's still not happy about me leaving at all."

"She's closer with you than she was with the last nanny." I think in part because Haley's not married. She doesn't have a husband she mentions, a whole other family. The lines were clear, last time.

Now the lines are so blurred I'm not sure they exist anymore. Haley was right: Penny might be young, but she does pick up on things. She's a smart kid.

Hopefully, my daughter's emotions will soon be rewarded.

The door opens and Deborah steps in. She smiles. "Am I on time?"

"Yup. She's upstairs, just had dinner, so you should be fine just to get her to bed and enjoy your evening. Feel free to sleep in one of the guest rooms if you're tired. I'm not sure what time we'll be back."

Haley frowns. "Where are you going?"

"We are going out."

"What?"

Deborah winks at me and then quickly disappears into the kitchen. "I'll just make sure the dishwasher's running."

It's painfully obvious, but I don't care. I'm too busy staring at Haley. "I wanted to give you a grand gesture. You're right. I have been jerking you around. I haven't committed to one thing or another. It's been... topsy-turvy in this damn household from the day you got here and a lot of that is my fault. But I know what I want, now, and I'm ready to take it."

I only just got back from work a short bit ago, so I'm still in my work clothes. "Let me change out of these, and then I'll take you to our first stop."

"Our first?" Haley folds her arms, but she's got an incredulous smile on her face. "What are the other stops? What are we doing?"

"I can't tell you, or it won't be a surprise."

I hurry upstairs to change into some worn jeans and a

black band T-shirt. They're the kind of clothes I wear on the rare nights I go out with my bandmates, but I think I'm going to start wearing them more often. Maybe even into the office. Who cares if I dress in a heavy metal T-shirt or show off my tattoos? I'm the CEO. I can wear what I want.

It's time to stop hiding who I am.

When I get back downstairs, Haley's eyes go a bit wide as she stares at the tattoos on my arms. I grin. "These still really do it for you, huh?"

She rolls her eyes, but her blush gives her away. "Just tell me where we're going."

"Nope. Follow me to the car."

I drive us into the city, to a tattoo parlor. I haven't been here in years, not since I got my last tattoo in memory of Emily, the hummingbird.

Now it's time for me to get a tattoo that represents something, someone, else important in my life: Haley.

We park and get out. Haley squints up at the parlor sign. "You're taking me... to get a tattoo?"

"Nope. I'm getting myself a tattoo. I want you here."

"To hold your hand?"

"And to give your input."

I can tell she hasn't put it together yet by the confused furrow in her brow. "Why?"

"Because the tattoo is going to be you."

Haley's eyes go wide and I grab her hand, leading her inside the parlor. The tattooist smiles at me as we walk in. "Hi, JJ, it's been a long time."

"Sure has been. Haley, this is Raven. Raven, this is Haley."

Raven smiles and holds her hand out. She's tall and covered in all kinds of tattoos, far more than I have, with bright blue hair tied in a braid. Haley shakes her hand. "Your tattoos are amazing."

"Thanks. Let's get your boy all set up here and we'll talk about the design. He gave me some ideas, but he said you were going to give some input as well."

We sit down on the chair and I take off my shirt so that we can find the best place to put it. A lot of my upper chest is covered, but there's room on my ribs and at my hips.

Haley looks concerned. "Won't it hurt? To get it there? It's basically just skin on bone."

"It will hurt more," Raven admits. "But I have plenty of people who get tattoos there who love them, and JJ here is experienced with the process."

"I can handle it," I promise.

"Here's the design we have so far." Raven gets her notebook and opens it to the page with the design on it: a stylized mongoose made out of musical notes.

"You love rock music," I explain. "And you remind me of a mongoose—they hunt down cobras and other dangerous animals without any fear, and you had no problem standing up to me from day one. I thought it represented who you are... and who you should be, because you deserve to have that confidence in yourself, always."

"He was very specific about the musical notes," Raven adds.

"Do they mean anything?" Haley asks.

I nod. "If you play them starting at the tail of the mongoose and work up to the nose, then they make a song. It's one I wrote years ago, just the melody. I never got around to figuring out the lyrics or even the full song because then everything happened with Emily. But the tune's stayed with me."

Now that I'm getting back to being in my band, I think

it would be nice to look at that song again. I think I could make it about Haley.

Haley's eyes well up and she sniffs, swallowing them down. "If you're sure...."

"Of course I'm sure." I take her hand and squeeze it.

By putting a tattoo of her on my body, I'm making her a part of me forever. I'm ensuring that she'll always be a part of my life. I want that, and I hope that in doing this, she's seeing that I'm ready to commit to her. To make her not my child's nanny, but my girlfriend, my partner, and hopefully even the proper mother of my child.

Haley takes my hand properly and sits down next to me. "I love the design," she tells Raven. "If JJ likes it, then let's do it."

"I do like it," I confirm.

Raven smiles. "Then I'll get to work."

There's something meditative about getting a tattoo. It's not comfortable, because you are in pain, but something about the pain—the level of it, how constant it is, the concentration of the tattoo artist—makes it like a background noise in your head. Your whole body just sinks into this state where you simply *exist*.

I can see why it becomes addicting to some people.

But Haley's got my hand, and now, it's not just meditative. It's something even more than that. It's this experience that we're doing together, something that's almost... sacred. It feels to me the way I'm sure my parents felt when we would go to church on Sundays. I never really understood it. I'm not religious that way, but my parents always felt like they were a part of something important by doing that.

Holding hands with Haley while I get this tattoo as she watches me get it, and we know it's for each other... that means a lot to me. It means something special and indefinable between us.

We're binding ourselves to one another, forever.

When the tattoo is finished, it's bandaged up, and I'm reminded of the care instructions to make sure my skin isn't damaged and the tattoo doesn't fade or need unnecessary touch-ups.

"You said that we had places to be," Haley asks as we leave the parlor. "Where else are we going?"

I check my watch and grin. "We're right on time."

"Right on time for what!?"

Mark told me about the place. It's taking place at a warehouse in the arts district: an underground battle of the bands.

Haley lights up as we walk inside, her smile broad enough to split her face and her eyes going wide. "An underground rock concert?"

"You're damn right." I drag her towards the middle of the fray, careful of the bandage under my shirt. "C'mon!"

She stares at me with awe in her eyes. Between this and the tattoo... well, I know that it's not a typical romantic gesture, but I hope that it's clearly romantic for her. I hope that she understands. This is who we really are, this is what we like to do, and I don't think she'd want the typical roses and a fine dining establishment. She likes "bad boys" and everything that comes with that, and damn it, that's who I am underneath the suit I've had to put on.

We get pretty close to the stage, and I get the pleasure of watching Haley rock out and lose her mind for a couple of hours as the bands play. They're all good bands, and it's a solid lineup, but I couldn't care less about the music. What I care about is watching Haley go bonkers, jumping up and down, screaming along, ecstatic and excited.

There's an intermission for the bands to get some water, people to take a break, and judges can start taking notes. Haley looks like she's on cloud nine. "You want a drink?"

"Yeah, c'mon." I grab her hand so we're not separated and lead her to the bar for a couple of shots.

Haley hops up onto the bar top, something that most bars would sternly reprimand you for, but not in a place like this. I step between her legs and she wraps them around me, her arms draping over my shoulders. Her body is warm and soft against mine, and at this level, her breasts are pretty much right at my mouth. The temptation to bury my face in them....

"Just water for me!" Haley yells over the crowd to the bartender.

I was hoping to do a little trick where I take my shot and then kiss her to feed her the alcohol, but it looks like Haley just wants to hydrate. Probably a good thing, with how we've been dancing along to the music, cheering and jumping up and down, stamping our feet.

We're given the water and Haley downs hers so fast that some of it leaks out the corner of her mouth, sliding down her chin, to her throat... between her breasts....

I lean in and lick at it. Haley stops drinking and whimpers, her hips rocking forward.

I take my water, have a couple of pulls from it, and then "accidentally" spill a little on her breasts again. "Oops."

Haley pants, her hands sliding into my hair, as I lick at her breasts. I can see her nipples through the soaked fabric of her shirt and I suck on one of them. Haley moans and squirms against me. "JJ... oh... please...."

I pull back. "You want to go somewhere a bit more private?"

Haley nods.

I help her down off the bar and lead her through the crowd. The music is starting up again, but I don't care. I'm more than happy to miss some of the bands if it means I get to bury myself inside of her.

We reach the bathrooms and wait as everyone hurries and rushes out, trying to get back to the music as the battle resumes. Then I grab the door and drag Haley inside, finding one of the bigger stalls and throwing the lock.

"Someone could walk in," Haley pants, even as she cranes her neck back to let me kiss her throat.

"Then they can turn around and walk out," I growl. I don't care if someone overhears us. This is a rock concert. What do people think is going to happen? This kind of thing is practically expected.

I lift her up against the wall and yank down her jeans as she palms me through mine. Her hand feels so goddamn good, massaging my aching cock. "You drive me crazy," I admit. "I want to fuck you all the time...."

I lick and suck at her breasts again and Haley moans. "P-please. Oh, *please*...."

"Would you like that? Hmm? Me just bending you over whenever I wanted? You like bad boys, you like men who can dominate you like that...."

I slide my fingers inside of her just to make sure she's ready. She's so fucking wet, holy shit. I finger fuck her quickly, rubbing at her clit, and Haley moans, writhing. "Such a good girl, so wet and ready for me all the time..."

"Yes, yes!" she pants. "I'm your—your good girl...."

"Just mine, right? Nobody else's."

"Just yours," Haley swears. "Oh fuck, please... fuck me—"

I pull my fingers out and line up my cock. I want her so

badly I feel like I'm going cross-eyed. "Yeah, don't worry, good girls get what they want, what they deserve...."

Haley moans as I slide inside of her. She feels so fucking good, so hot and tight. I thrust into her hard and fast, the two of us too keyed up after all of that rocking out to take it slow. Haley kisses me frantically, grinding down on me as I fuck her roughly.

She likes it a little rough, I've noticed that, but she also likes praise and being taken care of, and I know that none of her previous boyfriends ever did that for her. I'm going to do it for her. I'll be there for her, and I'll make sure that she never wants anyone else ever again.

"That's it," I growl. "You're mine, and you're going to come for me; you're going to come on my cock because nobody makes you feel as good as I do, isn't that right, sweetheart?"

"Yes," Haley pants. "Yes, I'm yours, I'm yours—please —*ah, ah, ah!*"

She comes hard around me and I groan, burying my face in her gorgeous breasts and coming inside of her, my hips jerking. She feels so fucking good. I wish I was younger so I could get hard again and fuck her a second time, right now.

We breathe together, swimming in the high of it all. After a moment, I set her down, then catch her as Haley's legs wobble, still a little shaky.

She smiles up at me. "Thanks."

I chuckle. "Of course."

I kiss her, and Haley moans into the kiss, melting against me. It feels so good to have her in my arms. "I never want to let you go," I blurt out softly.

Haley pulls back, frowning. "What?"

"What did you think tonight was, Haley? Just some big fancy send-off before you walk out of our lives forever?"

"I... I wasn't sure what it was," she admits. "I—I kind of hoped, but—"

"I wanted to woo you and treat you the way that you deserved. No more of this... fucking you out of nowhere and then acting like it meant nothing. No more claiming that it's not going to happen again. I wanted to show you how much I appreciate you. I wanted you to finally... for some guy to finally treat you the way that you deserve to be treated."

Haley swallows. "Jack... you... there's... there's something I have to tell you."

"If you don't want us to be together, then I understand. I know that this is a lot, and that it's scary. We've really gone about this all the wrong way. But I want to be there for you. I want to—"

"JJ," she interrupts me. "I have to tell you something. I'm pregnant."

My mind slams to a halt.

What!?

Chapter 23

Haley

O f all the things that I expected, Jack pulling out all the stops like this wasn't one of them.

He gets a tattoo that reminds him of me, that *represents* me. And he puts it on his skin forever, on his ribs in a vulnerable place. We hold hands the entire time. Then he takes me to an amazing concert, the kind of place that I love to go to, the kind of place I spent so much of my weekends at when I was younger? And we can't keep our hands off each other, of course we can't, but then he's saying all these sweet things and I....

Maybe it's the amazing orgasm, sweeping me away. Maybe it's the way Jack is talking to me, or the warmth in his eyes. But I suddenly can't handle the guilt of keeping this a secret from him. I need to tell him, no matter what.

"I'm pregnant."

Jack stares at me in shock.

"I know this might make you hate me." I can feel tears welling up in my eyes and I quickly pull away to grab some paper towels and clean myself up. "And I'm okay with that. But I couldn't... not tell you any longer.

"You're the first person who treats me well and actually has his life together. I know that you're not perfect. But after Reed and every other guy who was just... drinking away his money and cheating on me and being a lazy asshole... you're amazing. You treat me well, you really do, and I couldn't—I wasn't going to tell you because I don't want anyone to think that I—that I did this on purpose for your money."

"I don't care about your money, Jack, I really don't. I don't want anything from you, I don't want a single dime. I just couldn't let you—after tonight—I couldn't' let you go on without knowing the truth."

Jack stares at me for another moment, then clears his throat. He speaks slowly. "Is that... why you quit?"

"No. I found out afterward."

He nods. "So you wanted to quit for the reasons you told me."

"Yes."

"That's—that's fine."

"Fine?" I stare at him. Now I'm the one feeling shocked. "I tell you all of that and all you have to say is... fine?"

Jack nods, shortly. "Well, you clearly didn't want me involved, so, I won't be involved. I'll just let you leave and do your thing. It's what you wanted anyway."

I stare at him. "That's not—what?"

He cleans himself up. "I'll call you a ride to get you home."

"Jack—Jack!"

He exits the bathroom and I try to hurry after him, but once I leave, I'm immediately assaulted by a wave of people and noise. He's disappeared into the massive, writhing crowd, everyone jumping up and down and dancing and cheering. There's no way I can find him in this.

I stare at all of the people having a good time, blissfully unaware of how my heart was just broken.

What the hell am I supposed to do now?

Chapter 24

Jack

Haley's news is—it's—I'm—

I don't even know what to do or say.

An instinctive and horrible fear takes me over and I can only flee before I panic and stop being able to breathe.

Emily got pregnant, and it was supposed to be the best thing in the world—and instead, she died. She died and she left me to try and pick up the pieces of my heart.

If anything were to happen to Haley....

The very idea makes me sick, and makes me want to throw up. Haley kept it a secret from me and she was going to keep it a secret forever, and I don't know if I'm angry or if I don't blame her. I'm torn between both. I can see her side of things, but I also hate the idea that she wouldn't ever tell me, that there would be somewhere out there a child of mine that I didn't know about.

But all that aside... the fact that she's pregnant at all is just terrifying.

I can't lose another woman I love. I can't. I can't. I can't watch that happen. Not again.

I call Haley a ride and then I hurry home. I barely remember the drive. It's all a total blur in my head. I feel sick.

When I get home, I throw myself into the shower, shaking. There's no sign of Deborah, so I assume she's asleep in one of the guest rooms like I suggested, and I'm glad for that. I don't want her to see me like this.

I have to take some melatonin in the hopes of getting sleep, but I still don't feel rested when I wake up. I feel terrified. Sick.

Deborah's downstairs with Penny when I stagger down. She looks at me skeptically. "You okay?"

"I'm fine."

"Where's Haley?"

"She'll be in later as usual." Or at least I hope she will. She's got a few days left before she's supposed to stop working for me, but I wouldn't blame her if she decided to call in sick today, after what I just did.

I want to call and apologize, except I don't think that I could get my voice to work. That nameless terror seizes me again and I don't know what to do. I just knew that I had to get out of there.

"I don't suppose I have a business trip coming up?" I ask Deborah.

She frowns at me, and I know that she knows something's wrong. I'm not going to tell her what, though, and she doesn't ask. I suppose she's used to the strange back-and-forth between Haley and me at this point.

That's probably not a good thing.

"You could travel to Berlin in the next three days," Deborah says, her tone careful. "It would be just a couple of days, but I'm sure they would love to have you in person."

"Great. Book the trip."

Penny's scarfing down her food with one hand and reading with the other, and doesn't seem to be paying attention to whatever nonsense the grown-ups are discussing. Good. Let her keep her nose in a book. I don't want her to try and get me to take her on this trip too. I need to take some time to clear my head.

"I'm going to go get ready for work." I head out of the kitchen.

Deborah follows me. "Jack, is everything okay? You seemed excited last night and now—"

"It's nothing. I just need some time to get my head on straight."

"Head on straight about what? I thought you had it all sorted out."

"Well, I didn't have all the information."

Deborah frowns. "Listen, that woman is far too good for you. If you've done something to screw this up? Then I suggest that you fix whatever it is."

"Trust me, I know that she's too good for me. I've always been aware of that."

"Then what the hell is stopping you? What is going on?"

"I can't talk about it. Just book me the damn flights and hotel. And don't mess up the rooms this time."

Deborah's not fazed by my snappy attitude. "Whatever you say, sir." Her tone is cold, and, well... I deserve that.

I just need to get away and figure out what the hell I'm supposed to do.

Chapter 25

Haley

I steel myself to deal with Jack head-on when I show up at the house to get Penny. I'm not going to take this lying down. I'm not asking him for money or to be in our lives, but he can't set me up on this beautiful date and tell me that he wants to be with me, then flee once I tell him I'm pregnant.

But when I get there, I find Jack's gone.

"What do you mean, a business trip?" I ask Deborah while Penny hugs my leg. She's gotten especially clingy now that she knows I'm leaving and I can't blame her. I run my hand through her curls, careful not to tangle them. "He never said anything."

"These things come up quickly." Deborah's tone isn't very convincing, but I have the feeling she's not trying to make it be.

I lower my voice. "He's going to miss the recital."

Penny's school is putting on some performance thing that elementary schools tend to do about once a semester. The different classes have different things that they do, like a short play, a song, or a dance. Penny's been looking forward to it, especially because I think this is the first one that her father would've been going to.

Now, he's skipping it, and it's because of me. Because I told him about the pregnancy.

What the hell else was I supposed to do? I couldn't turn him down after he literally got a tattoo for me, and gave me this big night out; not without him getting suspicious. He deserved the truth of what was going on.

Now he's fled and I don't know what to do about it. I'm hurt, I'm disappointed, and I know that it's not my fault, that he's an adult who can make his own choices. But it still feels somehow like there's something I could and should have done differently to keep this from happening.

I take some deep breaths. There wasn't anything I could have done to stop Reed from cheating on me. How is this any different? Well, it's not as bad as being cheated on, that's fair, but I don't know that there's anything I could have done to stop Jack from running away, either. It was either lie to him or be honest, and I would rather have been honest.

Maybe we were just never meant to be together. Maybe he thinks I was trying to baby-trap him after all. Maybe the signs have been there the whole time. Everything keeps pushing us apart and making it harder for us; so really, I should just accept what the universe is trying to tell me and give up.

"He knows that," Deborah replies quietly. "He's sad about it. But he said he needed to get out of the area for a while."

Yeah. "I suppose she'll have more recitals." I smile down at Penny. "And I'll be there to see it. I'm really excited."

Penny beams at me. "I'll miss Daddy, but you're gonna be there! I can't wait to show you what we worked on!"

"I can't wait to see it," I promise her.

Deborah gives me a small smile. I try to return it, but I'm not sure how successful I am. I am excited to see Penny's recital because I love her, but I don't know how much of a good thing this whole situation can possibly be. In fact, I'm not sure how it could get much worse.

Spending time with Penny while Jack's away honestly feels like it did back when I first was hired, although I can't slip passive-aggressive notes under the door into his home office anymore. We play, we laugh, we have a good time, so I can't help but think about how easy it all is.

How easy it would be to think of her as my daughter.

I hate myself for wishing that this was my life. But now that I know I'm pregnant, it's like I can't stop feeling the potential growing inside of me, right alongside the baby. It would be so simple if I transitioned from nanny to wife, to mother....

But that's just how it feels when it's only Penny and me at the house. I know how it is when we go out into the "real world" and we have to deal with other people, people who will claim that I was just some young hussy who got knocked up. They'll claim I'm some kind of gold digger; and they'll probably even say terrible things about Jack too, about how he couldn't keep his hands to himself, and how all men are dogs.

The day of the recital arrives, and I dress up a little so that Penny feels special. Not as fancy as I got for the party, but I put on a dress and do my hair and some simple makeup. I want her to feel like this is a special occasion that's worth dressing up for.

We arrive and I drop her off so that she can go with her teacher and head backstage, and then I park the car and head to the auditorium to find a seat.

Just about every parent of a kid at the school is here. As the kids get older the parents stop coming to all of their activities. They miss sports games, play performances, competitions... but when the kids are young, the parents still make an effort to go.

It makes me sad. When I have my child, I'll make sure to keep going, even when they're a teenager. Even if they act like they don't care.

It's inevitable that I introduce myself to some parents because they're asking me who I am and whose kid is mine. I recognize a few of them from dropping off and picking up Penny, and some of them are even the parents of Penny's friends.

"Oh, you're Penny's?" one father asks me, shaking my hand. "I didn't know that Jack had remarried."

"I—"

"Oh, Penny talks about you all the time," someone else interrupts. She smiles at me. "You're clearly a great stepmom. I'm sure it's awkward—I'm divorced and I worry about how my kids will accept someone new—but I think you've done a great job with it."

"I'm not Penny's stepmother," I say quickly. "I'm the nanny."

"Haley!" One of the parents I know comes forward and hugs me. "It's so good to see you again. I see you're making friends already."

"I was just telling them I'm Penny's nanny." I gesture to the people I've been speaking with.

"We thought she was the stepmother," the divorced mom says, sounding embarrassed.

"Well, with the way that Jack's involving himself in Penny's life now more, can you blame us?" the first dad says.

"The guy never used to come to anything and now we see him around, he answers the PTA emails—"

"We thought he'd finally moved on," the mom finishes. She sounds disappointed that this isn't the case.

I'm surprised. These parents are a range of ages. Some of them are younger than I am, and some of them are Jack's age. But nobody seems to be batting an eye at the fact that they thought I was the stepmom and Jack's new wife.

"I'm sorry to disappoint you," I blurt out. "I didn't know that there was a misunderstanding. Penny and I are close, I love her very much, and I'm really glad to know that she's said nice things about me."

Everyone looks at each other, and then the conversation moves on. I can't interpret their faces. "What was that all about?" I ask the parent I actually know as we take our seats.

"Everyone was wondering for a while if you were the stepmom," she whispers back to me. "They were all hopeful. I know there are a couple of single moms who were sort of hoping to date Jack; I mean, who wouldn't want to date a handsome billionaire, right? But he's always been so curt and distant. We heard stories from the last nanny... anyway, he got so much happier once you started, we all kind of thought that... well."

"But you knew I was the nanny!" I hiss.

"That's what you said, but I honestly thought it might be just a cover! In case, you know, things didn't work out! It's hard dating when you have a kid, and what if you and Penny didn't click? I thought maybe this was a trial thing you guys were trying to make sure you and Penny bonded."

"And everyone was *happy* for us? I'm almost twenty years younger than he is."

"So? Why should we care?"

That brings me up short. This is a really good school, so there are rich parents here, some as rich as Jack, but others not nearly so much. I guess I assumed that everyone would judge the way the shareholders at the party had, but....

None of the teachers, all of whom aren't rich, have said anything, and none of the parents, no matter their ages or economic status, have said anything either. They all thought that I was dating Jack and they decided that it was none of their business, or they decided they were happy for us.

"Have I been kind of the problem too?" I whisper.

"Shh." The mom smiles at the stage. "It's starting."

Holy shit. Maybe I'm part of the problem.

Chapter 26

Jack

I hate that I missed Penny's recital, but I know it was good for me to take that trip for my mental health. Once I get back, I take her on a father-daughter date so that we can have some time for just the two of us.

Being away from Haley was both good and bad for me. It was good because it allowed me to think without being distracted by her actual presence. It was bad because I missed her, and I'm still really fucking afraid.

I love her. I'm in love with her. And I want to be with her. Going to Berlin only made that clearer than before. I missed her and Penny like they were extra limbs that had been chopped off and I hadn't even expected it to be that bad. I've traveled plenty for work in my time after all and I've never felt like I really missed home during any of that. But now? I just wanted to wrap things up and return to my girls.

Even if Haley isn't really "my girl" yet.

But the idea of committing to her and telling her how I feel and then... losing her like I lost Emily....

I couldn't go through that kind of loss again. I can't. Call me a coward, but it terrifies me, it makes some kind of pit open up in my chest and I'm in danger of falling through it into myself.

I get home, still with none of the answers I hoped this trip would give me, and instead with one little girl I have to apologize to for missing her performance.

"Haley recorded the whole thing!" Penny promises me as I take her to the bookstore. She's allowed to pick out as many books as she wants, and then we're going to get ice cream. "So you can see it!"

"I'm glad to hear it." I squeeze her hand. "I won't be going away so suddenly like that again, I promise. I will have to go away sometimes, but I think I can make sure that we know far enough ahead that I won't miss something important like that."

Penny nods. "Haley says you gotta take care of everybody in the company, like a daddy for everybody, and sometimes that means you gotta go fix stuff for them."

"Haley's right." And far, far too kind and generous with me. "But I'm still your daddy first, and I'm going to be making sure those two things don't get in the way again."

Penny nods solemnly. She's so scholarly and serious, it makes my heart ache.

I set her loose in the bookstore, and we read and buy a bunch of books, and then I put them in the car and take her to the ice cream shop.

"So, your birthday is coming up," I point out. "You're going to be six soon."

I can't believe it. It feels like yesterday she was born. Now she's going to be six years old. She's going into first grade next year, proper school at a desk and with homework assignments. She won't need a nanny in the same way, although she will still need one, and she won't have such a free schedule.

They really do grow up so quickly—and I missed the majority of those early years. I won't ever get those back.

I might be about to miss out on those early years with another child. I never thought of it that way.

Penny nods as she eats her ice cream. "I want a dinosaur birthday party!"

"We can definitely make that happen." I can just buy out the local natural history museum and we'll host the party in the dinosaur wing. I'm sure a generous donation as well won't go amiss. "Is there anything else you'd like? As a present?"

Penny pokes at her ice cream with her spoon. "I don't know, Daddy, it's a big idea."

"Well, hey, you know I can get you just about anything, right? If you want to go out to a dinosaur dig in Montana, or if you want to go to Paris, we can do that. The world is your oyster, sweetheart." There are very few things that money can't buy.

Penny chews on her bottom lip. "I want a mom."

My eyebrows fly up my forehead. "You want a mom?"

Penny nods. "I'm sorry."

"Why are you sorry?"

"I know you loved Mommy very much. Deborah says you loved her bigger than this." Penny spreads her arms wide.

"That's true. I did love your mom very much. You remind me of her, though, so it's like a piece of her is still with me."

"But she can't be my mom 'cause she's not here anymore. And I'd really like a mom. So I thought you could maybe love someone else?"

"Well, that's possible, but I don't know if I can manage that in time for your birthday. Your birthday's pretty close."

"Then you can ask Haley!" Penny says brightly.

"Haley?" I nearly choke on my own bite of ice cream.

Penny nods.

"What makes you ask for Haley? You want her to be your mom?"

"Uh-huh. I love my nannies. And I love Deborah too! We watch interesting movies when they babysit. They're all in black and white and people talk so funny. But I love Haley like... bigger than I love them."

"Gotcha."

"And you and Haley love each other," Penny adds, as if this is just a fact of life.

My eyebrows fly up again. This kid is going to give me a heart attack. "Oh?"

"Uh-huh. You guys make each other really happy. I like how you look at each other."

Even my kid can see it and she's not even six years old. "Are you... sure? You would want that?"

Penny nods. "I'm happy with you Daddy. But Haley makes us even happier."

It's so simple for her, as a child. It's so easy. And I'm not sure that she's *wrong,* either.

Maybe I've been making it more complicated than it has to be.

To Penny, her mother's death is sad, but there's nothing she can do to change it. She's not letting that sadness or fear hold her back. And here I am, being less mature than my five-year-old daughter.

I want to make my daughter happy, and this is what will do that. And she's right, being with Haley makes me happy too. Am I really going to deny my daughter what she wants because, what, I'm afraid Haley might die the same way Emily did? I'll sound ridiculous to Penny and when I think about telling her, I realize that it is ridiculous. I deserve better and so does my daughter.

Penny shouldn't be miserable just because I let fear win the day. And neither should Haley or me.

Chapter 27

Haley

I'm at home packing my things when the phone rings. It's Jack.

The temptation to ignore it is strong since I haven't seen or heard from him since he fled at the battle of the bands, but it could be Penny calling for some reason, or it could be important, and I'd rather make sure than be petty.

"Hello?" I answer with one hand while I keep packing. "Did I leave something at the house?"

"It's Penny's birthday party today."

"I'm aware." It's all she could talk about during my last couple of days with her. Then I left and I've been packing and getting ready to move my stuff down to my parents' house ever since. It's only been a couple of weeks without her, but I feel like someone's torn my heart out.

Every day the baby inside of me grows a little bigger, and the day grows closer when I'll be a single mother. My baby will have an adorable older sister and will never know, and Penny will have a younger sibling, and she'll never know.

It breaks my heart all over again every time I think about it.

"She really wants to see you. Could you come? Please?"

"I'm not going to come to a party and make nice like nothing's wrong," I snap. "You made it clear that you'll never actually commit to me, to us, and—"

"Just for Penny's sake, please. You don't have to stay long. You can even come a little early. The party starts at eleven at the Natural History Museum. Stop by a bit early and just hug her and say happy birthday. I know that I messed up. I messed up from the day we met. I have a lot of pain that I wasn't addressing this whole time and it kept hurting you, and I'm so sorry. But I don't think that either of us wants to let it hurt Penny. She doesn't deserve that. You've got every right to be angry with me, but she did nothing wrong and she shouldn't be punished for my bad behavior."

My heart sinks, because I know he's right. My issues are with Jack, not with Penny. Never with Penny. "I appreciate the apology."

"You deserved it. You deserve a lot more—a lot better—than what I've given you, Haley."

I sigh. "I'll stop by. Just to see Penny."

"Thank you."

I hang up and glare at myself in the mirror that hangs over my dresser. "You sap," I mutter. I really can't resist, can I?

I get myself out of my ratty T-shirt and sweats and into the shower, then brush my hair and put on a dress so Penny sees I made an effort for her. The Natural History Museum isn't a long drive from my apartment with Sara, and I'm able to get a bit more packing in before I leave to be there shortly before eleven. I don't want to run into other parents and awkwardly explain myself. I'm not sure if anyone even knows that I've quit, yet.

When I get to the museum, I'm shown in by one of the managers down the hall from the entry foyer to the dinosaur wing. There's a catering crew setting up the food, and a young man talking to Deborah at the far end of the hall, and then...

"Haley!"

Penny's dressed in a fairy dress and she rushes over to me, flinging herself at me. I crouch down and catch her so that I can give her a proper hug, holding her tightly. "Hey, sweetheart, how are you?"

"I missed you so much," Penny whispers, her voice choked. "But I knew you'd come here. I told Daddy what I wanted for my birthday and I knew he'd get it for me."

"You asked for me?" I'm bewildered and touched by her wish. I had no idea that she loved me that much. I love her, more than just about anything, and I know that she loves me, but this is still more than I ever let myself expect.

"No." Penny squeezes her arms tightly around my neck. "I asked for a new mom!"

I jerk back in shock and stare at her. "What?"

Jack clears his throat, and I look up. "So, I lied. The party is at noon, not eleven. I wanted to make sure that we had plenty of time."

I stand up and glance around. Deborah and the young man she was speaking to are gone, and so are the catering crew. What...?

Then Jack gets down on one knee and pulls out a small box.

My jaw drops and my hand flies to my mouth. Penny giggles, swishing her dress back and forth, clearly full of delight.

"I let my fear stop me from treating you right this whole time," Jack tells me, opening the box to show me a beautiful ring with a shining black stone inside of a diamond. The perfect kind of ring for a girl who likes bad boys and isn't the classically fancy type. "I couldn't commit to you or to my daughter. I kept letting things get in the way and stop me from doing what I always knew would make us both happy."

"But I'm done with that. Penelope wants a mother for her birthday and she wants her mother to be you, and I realized there was no way I could tell my daughter that the reason she wouldn't have you is I was scared of losing my happiness again. She would think it was ridiculous, and that helped me see how ridiculous it was. I want to be with you. So, Haley, will you marry me?"

"Well." My voice shakes and my eyes blur with tears. "You did get a tattoo for me."

I hold out my hand, my fingers shaking, and Jack slides the ring onto my finger. I finally let the tears fall as he stands up and takes me into his arms, kissing me.

Penny's hopping up and down like her body is too small to contain her joy. I turn to pull her into my arms too, the three of us hugging together. She's so happy she can't hold still, wiggling back and forth, giggling.

I still feel like I'm in a bit of shock, like this can't possibly actually be real. I look at Jack. "You're sure?"

"Haley, I wasn't myself for so much of my life. I was living a life of denying myself happiness, and I just got so used to it that I didn't even know what it was anymore. You called me out on my bullshit and you made me happy. I know you've struggled to feel like you deserve better and you've been treated like crap by the men you used to date, but you never lowered your standards to make it easy for me. You never let me get away with my bad habits or stay in my grief. You make me a better person. I love you and I want you with me. That's what I was trying to tell you about on our date when I got the tattoo. I wanted to tell you that I love you and I want to be with you."

My eyes well up with tears again and Jack tenderly wipes them away with his thumb. He smiles at me, his eyes radiating—radiating *love*.

I can't believe it. I just went from possibly the worst-case scenario to... to all of my dreams coming true.

I glance at Penny. "Should we tell her?" I whisper.

"If you're ready to," Jack says. He seems to understand exactly what I mean.

I crouch down in front of Penny. "I have a special birthday present for you," I tell her. "Would you like a baby brother or sister?"

Penny shrieks in delight and flings her arms around me again, and I hug her back, laughing. I look up at Jack and see him smiling down at us.

He looks so very happy—exactly how I feel.

Chapter 28

Jack

I'm in a meeting when I get the call. I look down at my buzzing phone to see that it's from Haley.

She knows not to bother me at work; she's very respectful about it, only texting if she has a question or something, and she knows I can get back to her whenever I have the chance. But she's due any day now, so if she's calling me—

"Excuse me," I tell the board. "I need to take this."

I stand up and exit the room, answering the phone in the hallway. "Hey, honey, is the—"

"Hi, Daddy!" Penny says brightly. "Mama can't talk on the phone right now. She's pushing the baby out!"

Oh boy. "I'm on my way right now."

Penny started calling Haley "Mama" almost right away. It was like she had wanted to call someone that all her life and she finally had permission. It makes my chest swell with joy whenever I hear her say it.

Haley's parents have come up to Seattle since it's so close to the due date, so I learn that Haley's mom is in the delivery room with Haley and that Haley's dad let Penny use her phone to call me. I promise I'll be there soon, and then I hang up and race to the hospital as fast as I can.

If I get a speeding ticket, well, the officer can just follow me to the hospital and I'll get it from him later. I have to be there for my wife.

Everything with the pregnancy has gone fine so far, but I'm still insanely nervous as I drive over and park. I race through the parking structure and into the hospital, finding the right room.

What if there was something that the doctors missed? What if Haley's actually had some concerns or pain but hasn't told anyone because she doesn't want me to worry and now it's too late? What if—

Penny and Haley's father are outside in the hallway. Penny beams as she stands up. "Hi, Daddy! You got here fast!"

"Sure did. I have to go in, where...?"

"Mr. Steele?" A nurse appears like she's been waiting for me. "Right this way, your wife's been asking for you."

I'm led into a room where I wash my hands and get covered up so that I'm sterile and won't accidentally bring in anything that'll make the baby or Haley sick, and then the nurse takes me to the delivery room.

I have to admit, I'm terrified. My stomach feels like it's going to climb out of my throat and vomit itself at my feet. But I can't let that fear get in the way as it has so many times before in my relationship with Haley. However scared I am right now, that's nothing compared to what Haley must be going through as she pushes this baby out and brings it into the world. I have to be there for her.

I swallow down my fear and enter the delivery room.

"JJ?" The moment Haley sees me, her face lights up. She looks exhausted and tears are sliding down her face, but she still reaches a shaking hand towards me. I take it and squeeze it hard.

"I'm here," I promise her. "I'm here, and you've got this. You've got this."

The delivery is intense, to say the least, and Haley is exhausted by the end of it—but I hold her hand and talk her through it. She pushes and she never gives up, and before I know it, our baby is being born, and the doctors are congratulating us.

"Everything's fine?" I ask. I can't help it.

The doctor hands the baby to the nurse, who cleans him off and hands him to me wrapped in a soft blue blanket. I hold him close—our son.

Haley smiles up at me tiredly, her eyes gleaming with joy.

"Yes," the doctor promises us. She smiles. "I know it probably didn't seem like it to you two, but that was a very smooth delivery. We're going to do a routine checkup on both the mother and the baby to make sure that everything's fine, but you both seem healthy to me."

Haley tiredly squeezes my hand. "See?" she whispers.

As usual, she's right.

The doctors make sure everything's okay and then Haley and the baby are wheeled into a recovery room, where Penny and everyone else can visit and see them.

Penny's wiggling with excitement as I carry her into the room. Haley smiles at her and holds out her arms. "Careful," I warn Penny as I set her down on the bed.

Penny snuggles up to Haley and I get our son out of the bassinet to show him to her. "Penny, meet your baby brother, Ben."

She reaches out a finger, and Ben wraps his little hand around it. Penny gasps in delight.

Haley smiles at me, and I smile right back. She's going to need a ton of rest, but she's okay. The doctors gave her a clean bill of health. Our son is okay, and there's nothing for me to worry about.

I don't have words for how happy I am. I kiss my wife on the forehead; so fucking grateful that I got this second chance at happiness. I almost messed it up so many times, but now I have the life that I always wanted: a life where I can be myself and embrace every part of me, from the band to the tattoos to fatherhood.

A life where I can be happy.

"Are you happy?" I whisper to Haley, just to make sure.

"I've never been happier," she promises me, and I kiss her again, just for that.

THE END

Thank you for reading ***Nanny for the Bossy Daddy***! If you loved this book, then you'll love ***Grumpy Billionaire Playboy***!

Continue on the next page to read the first chapter of *Grumpy Billionaire Playboy*!

★★★★★ "OMG! A must-read. I could not put this book down. The beginning of the book started a little slow, but once I got to Chapter 3 it got better & better. Even though they were enemies, their sexual compatibility was amazing. They were so great together & the chapter when Drake met Leila's parents was intense. The way he stuck up for Leila was so sweet! Will they have a happily ever after? Read this amazing book & find out."

★ ★ ★ ★ ★ "I've been getting tired of the grumpy billionaire friends to lovers brothers best friend trope but when I started this book I could not put it down. It blew me away. All the characters are well-developed, it is well-written and fast-paced. The protagonists Drake and Leila are steamy and sexy together. They learn about each other and are unafraid to admit when they are wrong. It is such a well-written novel I just loved it, even with all the tropes. Could not stop once I started it."

★★★★★ "OMG!!! This was another fantastic book and it was a page-turner and the suspense was WOW!!! It was addictive and I was at the edge of my seat and I could not even stop reading it or put it down for a minute. Leila and Drake's chemistry was like fireworks and their attraction was smoking hot. They could not keep their hands off one another they gave into their lust. They were falling in love with each other and how could they keep it a secret from her best friend? And how would her best friend feel about their romantic relationship? Could they have a happily after end after all? I guess you will have to read it for yourself. I highly recommend this book and you will not be disappointed at all."

Sneak Peak: Grumpy Billionaire Playboy

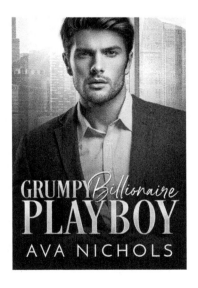

My brother's best friend is my worst enemy… Now, he's also my fake fiancé who just *took my v-card*.

Drake Bennet is a handsome, arrogant, Real Estate shark who always has women throwing themselves at him.

But I can't stand him; we've always fought and bickered growing up.

His mom has been badgering him to settle down, so he asked me to be his fake fiancé.

And I only agreed as long as he made me his plus one at exclusive events I needed to attend for my journalist job.

But while we're "pretending" to be engaged, Drake takes care of me in more ways than one.

His touch brings me to ecstasy for the first time and makes my body quiver from head to toe.

He's been caring for and protecting me in ways I've never seen before.

I'm falling for him, hard.

And if things couldn't get more complicated — **I'm pregnant.**

But this can't work. My new singing career is taking off and I'll be in the public eye.

And our fake engagement has to come to an end.

Or will Drake finally be ready for a "real" happily ever after?

Click here and get it now: *Grumpy Billionaire Playboy* - A Brother's Best Friend, Enemies to Lovers Romance

Chapter One - Leila

I clutch the folder of files in my hands as I walk along the office floor, trying to project confidence.

It's not that my story isn't good. I know it is. It's well-researched and timely, and I think I did a good job of being entertaining while also educating people in laymen's terms on the subject.

It's more that my boss is a stubborn jackass.

I reach her office and knock on the doorframe. "I'm here."

"Leila." My boss, Deirdre, smiles at me. "Come in. You said you had an article for the next issue?"

"Yes." I hold out the folder for her to take, watching as she flips it open. "It's a piece on independent musicians and how they're struggling in the streaming—"

Deirdre holds up a hand, cutting me off. "Leila." Her voice is stern. "How many times do we have to have this conversation? This is a lifestyle magazine, not the *New York Times*. We are here to give our readers the glamour and glitz that they pay for."

"But people want to make informed decisions about their lifestyle choices, like how they get their music and what musicians they listen to."

"Let me be even clearer." Deidre hands me back the folder. "You are here to cover social events. You are in an enviable position, with your connections...."

Ah, yes, my "connections." My parents are rich, just like their parents were, and their parents before them. I grew up among the affluent, so Deirdre exclusively gives me assignments covering the social events of the wealthy. I'm either already invited out of politeness, or I can score an invitation fairly easily, and it's better than sending in an "outsider."

Deirdre's also aware how much I hate these assignments.

I don't want to do fluff pieces, and I especially don't like going in and writing articles about who wore what and what was on the menu at social events held by people who trust me as one of them. It makes me feel kind of dirty. And what's the point, anyway? Who cares if we had mussels or escargot as the first course, and if the bride wore Vera Wang or Sebastian Paolo?

"This is what you're here to do," Deirdre finishes. "That's it. If I ever want something different from you, then I'll tell you. But until then, you do as you're told and cover the stories I tell you to cover. Is that understood?"

"Yes," I say, because I have no damn choice.

I need this job. It was difficult enough to get it in the first place, and while it doesn't pay a ton, it keeps all of my bills in order so I can live completely independent from my parents. I know they don't approve of my work, but honestly, that's the one part of my job that I enjoy: knowing how much they hate it.

But I can't afford to put my foot down and demand I be given more serious articles. This lifestyle magazine was the only place hiring a newbie like me, and it was a relief to have a regular gig instead of being an independent contractor for various online sites that got barely a dozen hits per article. Unless I want to go crawling back to my parents for money, I have to swallow my pride and do as I'm told.

Deirdre smiles at me. "Great. Now go and give the people what they want." She taps away on her computer. "Elizabeth Garner is getting married this weekend. I expect you to be there."

Elizabeth is one of the girls that I had to spend time with growing up because her father is a billionaire, and I got the invite to her wedding ages ago. I said yes, because I didn't know how to get out of it without a bunch of people making it a big deal and my parents throwing a conniption. But the fact that Deirdre just *expects* me to be able to go to this thing, last minute? What if I wasn't invited?

I know what she'd say. *Just make it work.*

Ugh.

"Sure thing," I say out loud, and I head out again. I know when it's okay to argue with Deirdre, and the answer is never.

On my way to the wedding over the weekend, I try not to get too damn depressed about my life. I'm independent from my parents, and that's the most important thing, or so I tell myself.

The wedding's upstate, a couple of hours from Manhattan where I live and work, and I pass the time by singing along with the radio. If I could actually go after any career I wanted, I'd be a singer, but I knew that was too big of a risk. If I failed, my parents would never let me hear the end of it. The likelihood of me actually being good enough to find success in the music industry? Slim to none.

Being a journalist isn't my first choice, but at least it's something I have a bigger chance in, and maybe I can actually find something about it that'll bring me a sense of success if I could just write about something more serious than the weddings of spoiled billionaire brats.

I finally get to the venue and pull into the parking lot. By that point, I'm rocking out to the radio, belting at the top of my lungs, fully lost in the moment. Nothing makes me feel better than when I'm singing. The whole world fades away and it's just me and whatever emotion the song is bringing me, whether that's joy, or anger, or heartbreak.

I hit the high note on the song, pumping my fist in excitement that I did it, keeping up with the crescendo and then ending the song with the performer, grinning in triumph.

The song ends and I turn off the car and the music, taking a deep breath. Okay. Time to stop enjoying myself and actually go in to face the music and deal with this.

This is what you're paid to do, I remind myself as I get up and leave my car. I just hope that it's all relatively painless and I can leave early after I get enough information for the article.

I walk through the parking lot and up the little path carved out through the grass. There are several archways set up, covered in fairy lights and flowers, announcing that we're entering the wedding of Elizabeth and Cayden.

I sigh inwardly. I wonder how much Cayden got to contribute to the wedding plans or if he just let Elizabeth do everything. When I get married, or rather if, because at this point who knows if a man will ever like me enough to marry me, I want my future husband to participate too. I want to make sure we have a wedding that is what he wants and not just what I want.

Or what my mom wants, but that's a whole other issue I'm not even going to consider in my imagination right now.

I get up to the front, where I'm not surprised to see a couple of men in black ties and suits standing at the entrance, checking people's invitations as they walk in.

This is why Deirdre has me go to these things. I'm actually invited, or at least theoretically I am. People in our social circle quickly get used to being papped, and having their private lives more or less plastered online, but sometimes they don't want that. Not because they care about privacy—if they did they could've managed to avoid being papped at all, as I have—but because they care about exclusivity.

You can't necessarily brag about your exclusive, amazing, showstopping wedding if everyone and their mother was invited. You need to show off by not showing off.

That's why I'm here. I give the people what they want,

because anyone else would be turned away if they're not a part of the inner circle.

I get up to the security guards. "Invitation?"

"One sec." I dig into my purse....

Oh no.

The guy sighs. "Ma'am...."

"No, I had it. Don't you have a guest list? I should be on there. Leila Douglas?"

"I'm sorry, but we can't let you in without an invitation," the security guard tells me, and my heart sinks.

I'm fucked if I can't get in there. My boss will kill me. As much as I gripe to myself about my job, I really need this and if I can't deliver on stories, then Deirdre will find someone who can and drop me.

What am I supposed to do?

"Any reason you're holding up my date?" someone says from behind me, and I jolt like I've been struck with electricity.

I turn around, hoping against hope that I got the voice wrong, but I know this voice. I've had to suffer through hearing that sexy baritone for most of my life.

Sure enough, there he is, and my heart sinks. Drake Bennet.

My mortal enemy.

Click here and get it now: *Grumpy Billionaire Playboy* - A Brother's Best Friend, Enemies to Lovers Romance

About the Author

Ava Nichols is a #1 Amazon Best Selling Author who writes relatable, sexy, and heartfelt contemporary romance. Her stories have a balance of fun, edginess, steam, light-heartedness and depth. You'll get to watch her characters grow, open up their hearts and eventually find a happily ever after.

Her favorite themes are Billionaire Bad Boys, Enemies to Lovers, Brother's Best Friend, Boss, Second Chance, and Age Gap.

When she's not reading or writing, she's enjoying nature, dance, pilates and spending time with her family. She lives in Southern California with her husband, two young children and two small dogs.

Join Ava's newsletter to receive a FREE copy of her book, *My Billionaire SEAL Protector*, plus news on upcoming releases, giveaways, free reads and more! https://BookHip.com/RSKPXRM

Also by Ava Nichols

Click here to see a list of Ava's other Bestselling books on Amazon!

Printed in Great Britain
by Amazon